Elliott W. Preston

Lord Byron Vindicated;

Or, Rome and her Pilgrim

Elliott W. Preston

Lord Byron Vindicated;
Or, Rome and her Pilgrim

ISBN/EAN: 9783744787963

Printed in Europe, USA, Canada, Australia, Japan

Cover: Foto ©Andreas Hilbeck / pixelio.de

More available books at **www.hansebooks.com**

Lord Byron Vindicated;

OR,

Rome and her Pilgrim.

BY

"And if my voice break forth, 'tis not that now
I shrink from what is suffer'd: let him speak
Who hath beheld decline upon my brow,
Or seen my mind's convulsion leave it weak;
But in this page a record will I seek.
Not in the air shall these my words disperse,
Though I be ashes; a far hour shall wreak
The deep prophetic fulness of this verse,
And pile on human heads the mountain of my curse!"
[*Byron's* " *Childe Harold* "; *Canto IV*; *Stanza CXXXIV.*

London:
SIMPKIN, MARSHALL & CO., STATIONERS' HALL COURT.
1876.

Index.

Introductory.

		Page.
Index to Illustrative Passages,	. . .	ix
Author's Preface,	. . . . .	xi
Motto Page, (Shakespeare),	. . .	xxv
Prose Dedication,	. . . .	xxvi
Poetical Dedication,	. . . .	xxviii
Motto Page, (Poe),	. . . .	xxxiii

Poem.

Rome,	. . . .	1
Rome,	. . . .	2
Rome,	. . . .	3

	Page.
Rome,	4
Greece,	5
Greece,	6
Greece,	7
Lucius Junius Brutus,	9
Lucius Junius Brutus,	10
Lucius Junius Brutus,	11
Lucius Junius Brutus,	12
Cincinnatus,	13
Napoleon,	14
Napoleon,	15
Napoleon,	16
Napoleon,	17
Appius Claudius -- Virginia,	18
Appius Claudius -- Virginia,	19
Appius Claudius -- Virginia,	20
The First Triumvirate,	21
Pompey,	22

	Page.
Pompey,	23
Julius Cæsar,	24
Julius Cæsar,	25
Julius Cæsar,	26
Julius Cæsar,	27
Mark Antony,	28
Mark Antony,	29
Passion,	30
Passion,	31
Augustus,	32
Augustus,	33
Augustus,	34
Religion,	35
Arians and Gnostics,	36
Athanasius,	37
Plato -- The Logos -- The Triad,	38
Jove and Semele,	39
Passion,	40

iv INDEX.

	Page.
The Human Mind,	41
The Human Mind,	42
Julian the Apostate,	43
Victories of Julian,	44
Victories of Julian,	45
Victories of Julian,	46
Victories of Julian,	47
Julian Proclaimed Emperor,	48
Jerusalem,	49
Rebuilding of the Temple,	50
Grove and Temple of Daphne,	51
Grove and Temple of Daphne,	52
The Palatine Hill,	53
Palaces of the Cæsars,	54
Charles Dickens,	55
Triumphal Arches,	56
Forum Romanum,	58
Fountains at Rome,	59

Page.

Night at Rome, ... 60

Canto II.

Coliseum, ... 63
Coliseum, ... 64
Coliseum, ... 65
Coliseum, ... 66
Coliseum, ... 67
Coliseum, ... 68
Coliseum, ... 69
Coliseum, ... 70
Coliseum, ... 71
Coliseum, ... 72
Coliseum. 73
Fame, ... 74
Fame, ... 75
Fame, ... 76
Fame, ... 77

	Page.
Love,	78
Love,	79
Love,	80
Love,	81
Love,	83
Love,	84
Night Thoughts,	85
The Poet's Prayer,	86
Byron,	90
Byron,	92
Byron,	93
Byron,	94
Byron,	96
Byron,	98
Byron,	99
Byron,	100
Byron,	101
Byron,	103

							Page.
Byron,	.	.	.	.	.	.	104
Byron,	.	.	.	.	.	.	105
Byron,	.	.	.	.	.	.	106
Byron,	.	.	.	.	.	.	107
Byron,	.	.	.	.	.	.	109
Byron,	.	.	.	.	.	.	110
Byron,	.	.	.	.	.	.	112
Circus Maximus,	.	.	.	.	.	.	114
Circus Maximus,	.	.	.	.	.	.	115
Circus Maximus,	.	.	.	.	.	.	116
St. Peter's,	.	.	.	.	.	.	117
St. Peter's,	.	.	.	.	.	.	118
St. Peter's,	.	.	.	.	.	.	119
St. Peter's,	.	.	.	.	.	.	120
Vatican,	.	.	.	.	.	.	121
Vatican,	.	.	.	.	.	.	122
Catacombs,	.	.	.	.	.	.	123
Words of Parting,	.	.	.	.	.	.	124

	Page.
Words of Parting,	125
Words of Parting,	126
Words of Parting,	128
Words of Parting,	129
Words of Parting,	130
Farewell!	131
Hymn to Mt. Blanc,	135
Hymn to the Ocean,	139

𝔏ist of
𝔍llustrative 𝔍assages
𝔔uoted from 𝔍oets and 𝔍rose 𝔍uthors in this 𝔙olume

1. BIBLE; *Galatians*, page 103; *Genesis*, 100; *Hosea*, 108; *Leviticus*, 108; *Psalms*, 108; *St. John*, introductory, xi; poem, 107; *St. Matthew*, 106, 113, 131; 1

2. BRYANT, (William Cullen); *"Battle Field,"* (The), 102; *"Thanatopsis,"* 127; . . . .

3. BULFINCH, (Thomas); *" The Age of Fable,"* 30, 39, 81, 90, 98, 101, 126; .

4. BULWER, (E. L., Lord Lytton); *"Richelieu,"* 99; . . . . .

5. BURNS, (Robert); *" To a Mouse,"* 104; . . . . . .

6. BYRON, (George Gordon, Lord); *"Childe Harold,"* Title Page; introductory, xii, xvi, xxvi, xxviii, xxx, xxxi; poem, 6, 17, 92, 107, 109, 121; *" Corsair,"* (The), 29, 76; *" Don Juan,"* 107; *" Dream,"* (The), introductory, xxvi; *"Giaour,"* (The), 8, 99; *"Island,"* (The), 85; *" Lament of Tasso,"* (The), 124; *"Lara,"* introductory, xxix; *" Lines on hearing that Lady Byron was ill,"* 109; *"Manfred,"* 35, 64, 72, 113; *"Marino Faliero,"* 100, 110; *"Vision of Belshazzar,"* (The), 16; 3

7. CÆSAR, (C. Julius); *"Letter to Rome,"* 43; . . . . .

8. COLERIDGE, (Samuel Taylor); *" Hymn before Sunrise, in the Valley of Chamouni, Switzerland,"* 31; . . . .

9. DICKENS, (Charles); *" The Ivy Green,"* 55; . . . . .

10. DRYDEN, (John); *"The Tempest,"* 11; . . . . . .

11. DU PAYS, (A. J.); *"Itinéraire de l'Italie et de la Sicile,"* 116, 118, 121, 123;

12. EDITOR, (The); introductory, xxx; poem, 75, 108, 114, 127; . .

13. EMERSON, (Ralph Waldo); *" The Problem,"* 76, 117; . . . .

14. GIBBON, (Edward); *"Decline and Fall of the Roman Empire,"* 36, 36, 37, 38, 41, 43, 43, 44, 45, 46, 46, 48, 49, 50, 51, 52; 1

15. GOLDSMITH, (Oliver); *"The Hermit,"* 128; . . . . .

16. GRAY, (Thomas); *"Posthumous Odes,"* 98; . . . . . .

17. HALLECK, (Fitz-Greene); *"Burns,"* 97; 1
18. HOLMES, (Oliver Wendell); *January (1876) "Atlantic,"* 10; . . 1
19. HORACE, (Quintus Flaccus); *"Odes,"* introductory, xxxv; . . . 1
20. KEATS, (John); *"Endymion,"* 91; 1
21. LONGFELLOW, (Henry Wadsworth); *"The Goblet of Life,"* 69; . . 1
22. LOWELL, (James Russell); *"The Present Crisis,"* 74; 1
23. MACAULAY, (Thomas Babington, Lord); *"Lays of Ancient Rome,"* 19;
    " Miscellaneous Essays," 92; , ... 2
24. MEREDITH, (Owen; Robert, Lord Lytton); *"Lucile,"* 130; . . . 1
25. MILTON, (John); *" Il Penseroso,"* introductory, xxix; poem, *"Paradise
    Lost,"* 83; 2
26. MOORE, (Thomas); *" Irish Melodies,"* 73; 1
27. OLMSTED, (Denison, LL. D.); *" Encyclopædia,"* 58; 1
28. PAYNE, (John Howard); *" Brutus,"* 10;. 1
29. POE, (Edgar Allan); *" The Coliseum,"* introductory, xxxiii; poem, 69;
    " The Raven," introductory, xxviii; 3
30. POPE, (Alexander); *" Essay on Man,"* introductory, xvii; poem, 41; . 2
31. ROGERS, (Samuel); *" Italy,"* 93; 1
32. SCOTT, (Sir Walter, Bart.); *" Reviews,"* 6, 73; 2
33. SHAKESPEARE, (William); *"All's Well that Ends Well,"* introductory,
    xxvii; *" Hamlet,"* 13, 20, 43, 99, 111, 123; *"Julius Cæsar,"* 24, 28, 61;
    "King Lear," 111; *"King Richard II,"* 31, 146; *"King Richard III,"*
    109, 113; *" Macbeth,"* introductory, xxv; poem, 27, 110; *" Merchant
    of Venice,"* 74; *" Romeo and Juliet,"* 127; *"Sonnet XXX,"* 129; . . 21
34. SHELLEY, (Percy Bysshe); *"Adonais,"* 104; *" Julian and Maddalo,"* 77,
    92; *" Queen Mab,"* 84; 4
35. SPENSER, (Edmund); *" Faerie Queene,"* introductory, xxx; poem, 31,
    114; 3
36. STERNE, (Laurence); *" Tristram Shandy,"* 106; 1
37. STOWE, (Harriet Beecher); *" Uncle Tom's Cabin,"* 111; . . . 1
38. SWINBURNE, (Algernon Charles); *" Chastelard,"* 125; . . . 1
39. TENNYSON, (Alfred); *" Morte d'Arthur,"* 36; *" Locksley Hall,"* 125; . 2
40. VOLTAIRE, (Marie Francis Arouet de); *Works of,* 91; . . . 1
41. WHITTIER, (John Greenleaf); *" Miscellaneous Poems,"* 110; . . 1
42. WORDSWORTH, (William); *" My Heart Leaps Up,"* 98; . . . 1

Author's Preface.

———•••———

"Greater love hath no man than this, that a man lay down his life for his friends." — St. John : Chap. XV ; v. 13.

I beg the favor of some explanatory words with the reader of the following pages.

I have willingly lain down my life for the noble Spirit whom I devotedly love. It is true I live to pen these lines, but the vitality, the strong principle of physical life has been lost, perhaps forever, in this cause.

Many will rejoice that my victory, if won, has been so dearly bought — many, too, I feel will sorrow, and to these I proffer my heartfelt gratitude.

If, by the sacrifice I have made, a great wrong be righted, and "The Pilgrim's" prophecy, after a lapse of more than half a century, find its predestined fulfilment in this generation, when scarce a single witness survives who can recall, in memory, that mighty Genius who walked for a brief space, as it were, "among them but not of them," I am repaid.

As with impaired and failing health I look back upon the Past, retracing the course that the voice of Conscience and of Duty impelled me to pursue, I find nothing there which I would change were I again to perform my weary but not ungrateful task.

One favor, only, will I request of my critics. Let them not misjudge this Preface, nor misrepresent the purpose of my work; for, as I hope for peace beyond those golden gates which seem not now afar, I have had no other motive in this than to defend a noble and innocent man against imputations I believe as unfounded as they are abhorrent.

It may be urged by mine enemies that the statement of acknowledged facts is not, properly speaking, a "Vindication." In the mere technical sense of the term this may be true; but in that far higher sense, wherein the appeal for Truth and Justice is carried before the tribunal of the heart, I claim that the title I have chosen is no misnomer. My purpose has not been to support, by legal proof, facts already accepted by the People, but to express, in language which shall bear the test of time, the convictions of the vast majority of the masses, both upon British and American soil.

I have unsheathed from its deep-rusted scabbard the once bright blade of Truth — a blade which has scarce been drawn since the valiant hand, now cold in Death, resigned its lingering grasp. He warred against Hypocrisy and Guilt in high places as in low: in the cause of Right, I, however unworthy, have dared to strike one more blow against the social Hydra he assailed and not in vain.

The general cry of Envy and of Malice, the portion of all truly great men, has died with that generation which has long since passed away; but it seemed reserved for this later day to furnish an example of that odious desecration of the memory of the dead, which, like the subtle venom of the serpent, tends to inoculate its victim with a virus as insidious as it is baleful in its effects.

The time is come when men refuse to believe so

cruel a tale attacking the honor of the poet who stands perhaps second only to Shakespeare amid the many Sons of Song that Britannia may proudly call her own. The great Spirit of Byron dwells with us but in memory, yet methinks that this memory alone should have evoked some voice to shield it from the mercilessness of a living assailant.

With such as these I waste no words; since

"Time! the corrector where our judgments err,"

will trace their lasting epitaphs — Futurity bestows her fadeless crown not on the merciless but on the just.

Numerous biographies have been written of

Byron, but few, if any, present a faithful portraiture of his wonderful, and in many respects unequalled, mind, with its multiform aspects, powers and capabilities — with its chameleon-like changes "from grave to gay," from the deepest pathos to the merriest mirth. I must however except from this class the "Life of Lord Byron" by Thomas Moore, (his loved and intimate friend), which, with few exceptions, forms a touching tribute to his noble and unaffected nature. Frank and artless as a child, when in the society of those in whom he had learned to trust and to confide, he unveiled to Moore much which was concealed from the world by the delicacy of a soul of almost unparalleled depth and sensitivity, which shrank from contact with the coarse and selfish natures by which it was surrounded.

One other pen has accorded yet fuller justice to the man as he appeared to those who knew him best; I allude to that of the late Countess Guiccioli, who was probably more intimately acquainted with the actual Byron than was any other person beside his beloved sister Augusta, and his friends Hobhouse and Moore. In her book, entitled "My Recollections of Lord Byron," etc., she has drawn the man as he appeared when freed from those murky vapors with which the malice of foes, the envy of inferiors and the voice of vulgar prejudice, strove to surround him. No juster nor more critical analysis of the character of Byron has yet appeared than the production of this distinguished and gifted lady.

The object of my work requires no further explanation than a reference to its title-page will supply.

As the question may arise, "why so large a proportion of the poem has been devoted to Roman History and monuments of ancient Architecture and Art?" I reply as follows:—

Firstly, because with the great subject of "Rome," the sympathies and interests of all educated societies must be forever blended; no subject, therefore, is better calculated to lend a lasting value to any meritorious effort which may treat of these magnificent ruins of the mightiest Empire of the Past.

Secondly, because no vindication of any person or persons, nor refutation of ungrounded calumnies — no matter how powerful, or just, such vindication may be — can, by itself, escape the character of a lampoon, and, as such, its chances of perpetuity of fame must be vastly inferior to those of the same matter when blended with a subject of undying interest, such as the past of "The Eternal City" certainly is. A coalition of this nature, if properly sustained, must confer a dignity upon the whole, which would otherwise be wanting in its parts.

Thirdly, because it was in Rome, amid those glorious relics of antique Art, that her unbroken but fainting "Pilgrim" pronounced the majestic prophecy of his future vindication, and triumph over relentless foes, which has given the fourth Canto of "Childe Harold" perhaps the very highest place among all poems of modern time.

The grand and rhythmical flow of the "Spenserean Stanza" (the measure likewise of "Childe Harold"), has been of inestimable aid to me in my work, despite the difficulties of its mechanical construction, from the harmony existing between the thought and its form of expression. It seems, indeed, peculiarly adapted to those subjects which must necessarily combine dignity of style with force of diction.

I have finished: if this, my work, be worthy, it will live — if unworthy, it must fall; — that Truth may prove triumphant is the prayer of

— " his virtues
Will plead like angels, trumpet-tongued, against
The deep damnation of his taking-off;
And pity, like a naked, new-born babe,
Striding the blast, or heaven's cherubim, horsed
Upon the sightless couriers of the air,
Shall blow the horrid deed in every eye,
That tears shall drown the wind."
[Shakespeare's " Macbeth:" Act I; Scene VII.

Prose Dedication.

TO the memory of her with whose welfare the gentlest sympathies and affections of that noble Being, it is the purpose of the present poem to place in his true light before the world, were inseparably blended, I inscribe this humble offering at the shrine of eternal Truth — to her whom the poet describes as

"Ada! sole daughter of my house and heart!"

["*Childe Harold :*" *Canto III.*]

With this fair offspring of an ill-starred alliance his brightest hopes were forever united; she was, with the exception of a beloved sister, the only living thing to which his tortured heart could turn in its dark and bitter hours of solitude and bereavement.

About this beautiful child, Byron's deep and passionate nature twined its tendrils of affection with an intensity of feeling few may either fathom or understand; she was as his own words most aptly express, but with regard to another,

"The ocean to the river of his thoughts, which terminated all:" etc.

["*The Dream.*"]

In exile it was to his absent darling that his seared but loving heart ever turned, with fond and ungovernable yearnings.

It is meet, therefore, that this strain whose aim it is to dispel forever those shadows which Bigotry, Misconception, Envy and Malice, have cast about the fame and fortunes of Byron — that surpassing Genius whose gigantic intellect dwarfed and dwindled the galaxy of lesser stars surrounding him — it is meet this tardy, but perhaps not all unworthy, retribution should bear the name and sanction of that sweet daughter whose young life was shortened by the knowledge of the cruel persecution which drove *him* forth, who should have shone the "bright, particular star" of his native land, to be a wanderer upon the face of the earth and a stranger amid strangers.

To the memory of that "Ada," (the late Lady Lovelace), with sentiments of the deepest reverence and respect, I dedicate this vindication of her injured father's memory.

THE AUTHOR.

𝔓oetical 𝔇edication.

𝔗o 𝔄da.[1]

"ADA! sole daughter of my house and heart!"[2]
Nay! not of mine — of one more doubly dear,
Through whose high destinies thou play'd a part,
Inseparably blended — everywhere
Pledge present through all absence! let me here
Invoke thy sunny Spirit by the shame
Done thy defenceless sire; [3] and if a tear
Bedim, the while, this eye, thou wilt not blame,
Nor deem it Woman's weakness which thus hail'st thy
name!

---

(1) The late Lady Lovelace, daughter of Lord Byron.
(2) *Byron's* " *Childe Harold:* " *Canto III; Stanza I.*
(3)   —— " unmerciful Disaster
Followed fast and followed faster
Till his songs one burden bore —
Till the dirges of his Hope that

Ṭo Ạda.

'TIS a sad tear of Sorrow, link'd with Love;
Sorrow for him — Love for his cherish'd child!
Thou tender nursling, timid as the dove,
Heiress of his starr'd (¹) Spirit, unbeguiled
By those who would have warp'd thee and defiled
Thy father's mem'ry! I would fain entwine
Thy name with this, my lay — so be it styled
Thy song, sweet girl, and as a spell divine
That thought shall mould my strain — e'en lighten (²)
through each line! `

Melancholy burden bore
Of 'Never — nevermore.' "
[*Poe's* " *Raven.*"

(¹) " Or that *starr'd Æthiop* queen," etc.
[*Milton's* " *Il Penseroso.*"
(²) " And the wild sparkle of his eye seem'd caught
From high, and *lighten'd* with electric thought," etc.
[*Byron's* " *Lara :* " *Canto I.*

𝕿𝖔 𝕬𝖉𝖆. (¹)

THEN wherefore blindly weep — Thou be'st but blest
In far escapement from Eld's (²) earthly ill! (³)
Love warmly wooes thee! — leave that rapturous
    rest
To weave fond fancies which would work thy
    will! —
They tempt thee from thy fold, thus to fulfill
Pure Virtue's prayer! Nor need I plead in vain —

(¹) [It will be noticed that the alliteration of this stanza is perfect — being either double, triple, quadruple, quintuple or sextuple, in each line; no individual line being required a second time in order to furnish from the stanza all the above-mentioned alliterations. — E.]

(²) Old Age.

(³) " And with the ills of *Eld* mine earlier years alloy'd."
            [*Byron's " Childe Harold : " Canto II : Stanza XCVIII.*
" As feeling wondrous comfort in her weaker *eld :* " etc.
            [*Spenser's "Faerie Queene:" Book I; Canto X.*

A magic spell surrounds me, soft and still,
Freighted with Inspiration, while I fain
Would greet its gentle birth which melts in Beauty's
main! (¹)

(¹) As a fitting concomitant to the foregoing lines of invocation for inspirational aid — addressed to the bright and changeless idol of Byron's devotion — I append his own eloquent declaration of that one absorbing passion which no mortal pen, save his alone, could so exquisitely portray : —

" Is thy face like thy mother's, my fair child!
ADA! sole daughter of my house and heart?
When last I saw thy young blue eyes they smiled,
And then we parted, — not as now we part,
But with a hope. —
                Awaking with a start,
The waters heave around me; and on high
The winds lift up their voices : I depart,
Whither I know not; but the hour's gone by,
When Albion's lessening shores could grieve or glad
mine eye.
                *   *   *
" My daughter! with thy name this song begun —
My daughter! with thy name thus much shall end—
I see thee not, — I hear thee not, — but none
Can be so wrapt in thee; thou art the friend
To whom the shadows of far years extend :
Albeit my brow thou never should'st behold,
My voice shall with thy future visions blend,
And reach into thy heart, — when mine is cold, —
A token and a tone, even from thy father's mould.

" To aid thy mind's development, — to watch
Thy dawn of little joys, — to sit and see
Almost thy very growth, — to view thee catch
Knowledge of objects, — wonders yet to thee!

To hold thee lightly on a gentle knee,
And print on thy soft cheek a parent's kiss, —
This, it should seem, was not reserved for me;
Yet this was in my nature : — as it is,
I know not what is there, yet something like to this.

" Yet, though dull Hate as duty should be taught,
I know that thou wilt love rue; though my name
Should be shut from thee, as a spell still fraught
With desolation, — and a broken claim :   [same,
Though the grave closed between us, — 'twere the
I know that thou wilt love me; though to drain
My blood from out thy being were an aim,
Still thou would'st love me, still that more than life
retain.

" The child of love, — though born in bitterness
And nurtured in convulsion. Of thy sire
These were the elements, — and thine no less.
As yet such are around thee, — but thy fire
Shall be more temper'd, and thy hope far higher.
Sweet be thy cradled slumbers! O'er the sea,
And from the mountains where I now respire,
Fain would I waft such blessing upon thee,
As, with a sigh, I deem thou might'st have been to me."

[Byron's "Childe Harold:" Canto III; Stanzas I, CXV, CXVI, CXVII, CXVIII.

" ' We rule the hearts of mightiest men — we rule
With a despotic sway all giant minds.
We are not impotent — we pallid stones.
Not all our power is gone — not all our fame —
Not all the magic of our high renown —
Not all the wonder that encircles us —
Not all the mysteries that in us lie —
Not all the memories that hang upon
And cling around about us as a garment,
Clothing us in a robe of more than glory.' "

[*Poe's "Coliseum."*

Lord Byron Vindicated;

OR,

Rome and her Pilgrim.

———◦◦◦———

CANTO THE FIRST.

———◦◦◦———

"Sic est: acerba fata Romanos agunt,
Scelusque fraternæ necis;
Ut immerentis fluxit in terram Remi
Sacer nepotibus cruor."

[*Horace: Lib. V; Ode VII.*

Lord Byron Vindicated.

CANTO THE FIRST.

Rome.

TITANIC Mother! whose heroic race,
   Nurtured in arms, first birthright of the soil,
Conquer'd unconquer'd Nations! where *their* place
And *thine*, dismantl'd mourner? Of their toil
The arch'd memorial from the Victor's spoil
Alone remaineth, and the ivied wall
Telleth all Time thy glory whose recoil
Mankind bewaileth with thee, for thy fall
Hath shatter'd unborn Empires waiting but thy call!

𝕽𝖔𝖒𝖊.

WHERE now thy vanish'd glories, and the Car
    Wherein th' empurpl'd Victor met the gaze
    Of Rome's free populace, when, from afar,
    The trump announc'd the Triumph's splendid
      blaze?
    Where, where are these? O, light of latter days!
    Can'st thou not pierce the shadows of their tomb,
    And rouse yon mighty phantoms?—Lo! their bays
    Bloom with perennial freshness, for the Womb
Of Earth claims not their *Spirits* which all Time
      illume!

CANTO I.

Rome.

THE pilgrim still revisits thy lone halls
And lonelier altars, where the Pagan throng
Flock'd to fantastic worship which appalls
The later Christian! Say! was it a wrong,
This Pantheistic shadow? Was their song
Meant not to worship Nature? Yea! the sense
Of high Omnipotence was theirs; the thong
Which bound their Reason was a spell intense,
Fraught not with Crime, but Error, and a just defence

𝕽𝖔𝖒𝖊.

'G AINST Atheistic tenets which deny
　　Aught save a soulless Law which darkly guides
　　This million-orb'd Creation, or defy,
　　To proof, the Soul's existence which abides
　　In inner Consciousness whose secret tides
　　Teem with immortal Reason!　Was it not
　　A just Religion, and is he,who prides
　　Himself on riper wisdom and a lot
Cast in a brighter day, to deem God was forgot?

CANTO I.

𝕲𝖗𝖊𝖊𝖈𝖊.

WHEN, from her tripod, the pale Pythoness (¹)
   Evolv'd the scheme of Empires, in the mind
Of Greece thy glories dwelt not!— If Distress
Were canopied above her 'twas a kind
Of natural Retribution, for we find
Each star's dim declination doth succeed
Its too meridian splendour!— God design'd
Man in His holy image, yet decreed
The doom of guilty Sodom to the Serpent's seed!—

(¹) A name given to the Priestess of the Delphic Oracle.

𝕲𝖗𝖊𝖊𝖈𝖊.

A ND what, forsooth, hath been this serpent seed?
The hateful lust of Power, and those things
That do debase our natures. Have we need
To yield those mightier prospects which the wings
Of bright Intelligence may mount, where rings
A psalmody whose whispers fall like strains
Of most celestial music? Ah! there clings,
Despite Man's degradation, the remains
Of bright Remembrance which Earth's fetters still dis-
    dains! (¹)

(¹) "Spurning the clay-cold bonds which round our being cling."
                        [*Byron's " Childe Harold:" Canto III; Stanza LXXIII.*

The resemblance which may be traced between these passages is accidental, so far as plagiarism is concerned. It is, perhaps, not remarkable that the sub-lime sentiments pervading a poem like "Childe Harold" should make a pro-

CANTO I.

Greece.

Y ET Greece! Fair Greece! if that thy hope were
    marr'd
By mockeries like these — if a dark fate
Bound thee in its fell bands until thy starr'd,
High destiny succumb'd, I will not prate

---

found and lasting impression upon the mind, and more particularly so with one
whose existence passes, for the greater part, in an ideal world: such is the Poet.
During the composition of this poem the author has purposely refrained from
the perusal of such portions of "Childe Harold" as bore more particularly
upon his own theme; nevertheless, *accidental* resemblances may doubtless be
discovered in the sentiment, but never in the words unless acknowledged by
marks of quotation. It would, indeed, be more singular did the seed sown long
since in the Mind's fertility yield no return after its long incubation, and more
especially when one's powers are concentrated in the production of a somewhat
similar poetical composition. Regarding any possible charge of plagiarism I can
do no better than append the words of Sir Walter Scott : —

"It is a favorite theme of laborious dullness to trace such coincidences, because
they appear to reduce genius of the higher order to the usual standard of humanity, and of course to bring the author nearer to a level with his critics."

The worn and oft-told moral, nor dilate
On that which might have been had'st thou for-
   sworn
Unnatural Ambition — the deep Hate
'Twixt Athens and brave Sparta: though we
   mourn
Thy sad and early fall, 'tis much that thou wert
   born! ([1])

([1]) " Clime of the unforgotten brave !
Whose land from plain to mountain-cave
Was Freedom's home or Glory's grave !
Shrine of the mighty ! can it be,
That this is all remains of thee?
*   *   *   *   *   *   *
'Twere long to tell,and sad to trace,
Each step from splendour to disgrace ;
Enough — no foreign foe could quell
Thy soul, till from itself it fell ;
Yes ! Self-abasement paved the way
To villain-bonds and despot sway."   [*Byron's "Giaour.'*

CANTO I.

Lucius Junius Brutus.

BRUTUS, the first of Consuls! in thy name
    Nobility seems centred! When the slave,
    Black-hearted Sextus, won a felon's fame,
    And wrong'd Lucretia sought within the grave
    To hide her Soul's dishonor — when the wave
    Of Rome's wide indignation pour'd a flood,
    And proved the Sibyl of the mountain cave,
    Then, *thou* did'st scourge from thence the scorpion
        brood,
And, midst Fame's noblest sons, a mightier hero stood!

𝕷𝖚𝖈𝖎𝖚𝖘 𝕵𝖚𝖓𝖎𝖚𝖘 𝕭𝖗𝖚𝖙𝖚𝖘.

THE Sibyl spake — "*A fool shall set Rome free!*"(¹)
Oh, noble Brutus! in thee Time fulfill'd
Her ancient prophecy! Oft, oft we see
Slight means speed mightiest ends; the proudly
    skill'd
Are not His chosen instruments; instill'd
In simplest bosoms seems prophetic store
Which acts through Inspiration; (²) they that build
But on their gather'd wisdom err the more: —
Not from the brain, but *heart*, flow'd Shakespeare's
    matchless lore! (³)

(¹) " The race of Tarquins shall be kings
Till a fool drive them hence and set Rome free ! "
       [*Payne's " Brutus : " Act I; Scene III.*
(²) " No will of your own with its puny compulsion
Can summon the spirit that quickens the lyre ;

CANTO I.

𝕷𝖚𝖈𝖎𝖚𝖘 𝕵𝖚𝖓𝖎𝖚𝖘 𝕭𝖗𝖚𝖙𝖚𝖘.

P ARENT, but sterner Judge! On that fell night
   When Treason leagued with the Etrurian foe,
Amidst the outlaw'd band, in thy fond sight
Shamed and undone did thy twin nurslings show!—
Then was thy great heart bow'd — each bitter throe
Pleading a father's nature!—sternly just,
The horrid sentence fell, but hoarse and low,
Whilst they that listen'd quail'd — the awful trust
Fulfill'd, thy Spirit sank all prostrate in the dust!

It comes, if at all, like the Sibyl's convulsion
And touches the brain with a finger of fire."
        [*Holmes, in January "Atlantic,"* 1876.
(¹) [Note to page 10.]
"But Shakespeare's magic could not copied be;
Within that circle none durst walk but he."
        [*Dryden's " Tempest: " Prologue.*

𝕷𝖚𝖈𝖎𝖚𝖘 𝕵𝖚𝖓𝖎𝖚𝖘 𝕭𝖗𝖚𝖙𝖚𝖘.

FOR thee the pious matron mourneth long
In sackcloth and in ashes, whilst the tone
Of Revelry is hush'd — the happy song
Dies on the whisp'ring wind!—thou who alone
Wert Heaven's chosen instrument, when grown
To an unjust proportion Royal Law
O'erstepp'd the bounds of Freedom whose fair
    zone
Admits no base curtailment, art no more: —
Sleep, noble Brutus! Rome reveres the name thou bore!

CANTO I.

𝕮incinnatus.

" GIVE me that man that is not Passion's slave!" (¹)
   Thus spake the Danish Prince with satire keen.
Hail, Cincinnatus! borne o'er Adria's wave
To every clime hath thy discretion been;
Thy name hath grown a watchword, and the scene,
  The theatre of Glory which thou trod,
Awhile its chiefest actor, with a mien
  Where majesty and grace bespoke the God,
May boast no loftier son than he who till'd her sod!

(¹) *Shakespeare's* " *Hamlet :* " *Act III; Scene II.*

𝔑apoleon.

T HE Ploughshare and the Sword ! Ill-mated pair,
Forged of a kindred steel to serve or slay
By Man, Creation's tyrant, whose chief care
Hath ever been to blight his brother's day
With Fire, Rapine and Slaughter — to obey
The tiger's native instinct; — such was he,
The modern Gallic Cæsar, who did prey
'Pon Europe's wretched millions, 'mid a sea
Of Carnage, till he fell by Fortune's just decree!

Napoleon.

WHENCE springs this thirst for Slaughter which
    hath lain
Earth's proud and populous Nations prone in
    dust —
Which gloats above the mountains of the slain,
Or revels in the Conqueror's sateless lust?
Napoleon! such wast thou! Though urn and bust
Groan 'neath thy gather'd greatness, Time shall
    tell
Thy guilt-emblazon'd story; and the crust,
The bitter bread of Poverty whose hell
Engulfs the wretched Starveling—those lost Souls that
    sell

Napoleon.

THEIR birthright of salvation — bitterer grow
    That *thou* hast warr'd and wasted! Yea! thy name
Be coupled with a curse, for thou did'st sow
The seeds of Desolation, whence thy fame
Shall reap a thistle-harvest where the shame
Shall choke thy blooming Glory! 'Pon thine urn,
As in Belshazzar's hall of yore, in flame
Is traced a destiny! — The letters burn, [learn! (¹)
Whereon Mankind shall gaze, and thy dark lesson

(¹) " In that same hour and hall,
        The fingers of a hand
    Came forth against the wall,
        And wrote as if on sand :
    The fingers of a man ; —
        A solitary hand
    Along the letters ran,
        And traced them like a wand.
    ✦   ✦   ✦   ✦   ✦   ✦

" Belshazzar's grave is made,
        His kingdom pass'd away,
    He, in the balance weigh'd,
        Is light and worthless clay.
    The shroud, his robe of state,
        His canopy the stone ;
    The Mede is at his gate !
        The Persian on his throne ! "
    [*Byron's " Vision of Belshazzar."*

𝔑apoleon.

N ONE doubt thy matchless Genius — It was such
   As might have made this world a worthier place
For Man's probation, and thy Midas touch (¹)
Transform'd to gold, not *ashes*, his weak race;
But thine ensanguin'd hand forbore to trace
In brighter characters and loftier line,
The name of " Benefactor " — Thy disgrace
Must ever be thou *could'st* but *would'st not* twine,
With   aught   save   blood-bought   laurels,   Nature's
   bright design! (²)

(¹) Midas, the fabled king of Phrygia: his miraculous power of turning all
he touched to gold is too well known to require mention.

        (²) "The fool of false dominion — and a kind
            Of bastard Cæsar, following him of old
            With steps unequal; for the Roman's mind
            Was modell'd in a less terrestrial mould,
            With passions fiercer, yet a judgment cold,

Appius Claudius -- Virginia.

NOW mark the base Decemvir who betray'd
A Nation's trust, and shamed the Roman crest!
False Appius! well the Gods aveng'd the shade
Of fair Virginia!—The lone father press'd,
For the last time, the virgin to his breast,
Whilst the avenging Furies' cheeks were wet,
Yet once again, with tears! (¹) The Titans rest
From strife in Tartarus! Fate's seal is set, [yet!
And dread Nemesis (²) hastes, ne'er balked of Justice

And an immortal instinct which redeem'd
The frailties of a heart so soft, yet bold,
Alcides with the distaff now he seem'd
At Cleopatra's feet, — and now himself he beam'd."
        [*Byron's " Childe Harold :" Canto IV; Stanza XC.*

(¹) The *first* time this phenomenon occurred is said to have been when
Orpheus sought his Eurydice in the Stygian realms, moving all hearts by the
witchery of his melting strains.

(²) The avenging Goddess of ancient Rome.

Appius Claudius -- Virginia.

SHE was the fairest flower of thy fair clime,
O, sunny land of Italy! — the bride,
To be, of fond Icilius — in sweet prime
Of Youth and budding Beauty — the just pride
Of a free Roman's heart, which, when denied
Impartial Justice, snatch'd the ready knife,
And smote with desp'rate hand; yet, ere she died,
Arose a mighty shout — a sound of strife
That shook the massy walls, and doom'd the Tyrant's
     life! (¹)

(¹) " With that he lifted high the steel, and smote her in the side,
And in her blood she sank to earth, and with one sob she died.
           *   *   *   *   *   *   *
And in another moment brake forth from one and all
A cry as if the Volscians were coming o'er the wall."
                              [*Macaulay's " Lays of Ancient Rome."*

Appius Claudius -- Virginia.

OH, dark, unholy deed! A father shed
The parent stream that flow'd within his breast,
To save his lamb from the Adult'rer's bed!
Ha, Appius! 'tis the headsman thou hast prest,
Couch'd in the damp vault's gloom! Pois'd o'er
    thy crest
Trembles the glittering glaive! Before thy sight,
See! See! the bloody knife, wan Murder's guest,
Tents (¹) the rack'd Conscience till the hollow
    Night
Teems populous with phantoms, as fair Day with light!

(¹) Tents — pierces. — " I'll *tent* him to the quick; " etc.
    [*Shakespeare's " Hamlet:" Act II; Scene II.*

𝕿𝖍𝖊 𝕱𝖎𝖗𝖘𝖙 𝕿𝖗𝖎𝖚𝖒𝖛𝖎𝖗𝖆𝖙𝖊.

W HERE sleep the first Triumvirs? (¹) Is there
aught
To mark their resting place? Yon shaft upbears
Awhile the fame of Pompey, but inwrought
On Hist'ry's page, which Time nor Spoiler wears,
Is graved a lasting tablet, nor the prayers
Of Hate nor Malice, nor the arm of Power,
Which mars material records, here prepares
A forc'd oblivion! — their immortal dower
Is writ upon Fame's page, unto Time's latest hour!

(¹) The body of Cæsar was burned in the Forum, near the spot where may still
be traced ancient remains of his famous rostrum. It was to this rostrum that the
head of the great Cicero was affixed by the order of Mark Antony. Pompey
fled into Egypt a miserable fugitive. Well may we ask, turning from their ever-
green memories to their scattered dust, "Where sleep the first Triumvirs?"

Pompey.

WHERE sleep the first Triumvirs?   The far shore
Of Nile-fed Egypt did receive the corse
Of fallen Pompey — he who proudly bore
.Victorious Eagles where Rebellion's source
Rose, dark and threat'ning!   Conscience nor
    Remorse
Impell'd the guilty deed — He darkly died
By the Assassin's knife!   In his sole loss
All Rome was widow'd!   He, who late defied
Proud Syria's serried host, is now a tomb denied!

𝔓𝔬𝔪𝔭𝔢𝔶.

T RUTH! 'twas a tardy Justice that uprear'd
   Unto the injur'd Pompey the proud stone, (^{1})
   Less glorious than his fame which huge appear'd
   To his abased detractors!—They, alone,   .
   Might tremble at his greatness! To atone
   His wrested sceptre did he not subdue
   Th' ambitious chief of Pontus, haughty grown,
   Foe of the Roman State, and wider drew
The broad'ning bands of Empire, smiling as they grew?

(^{1}) " Pompey's Pillar."

𝕵𝖚𝖑𝖎𝖚𝖘 𝕮æ𝖘𝖆𝖗.

A ND he, the first great Cæsar! who prepared
The way to future Conquest, and who fell,
Bathed in the tears of Rome!—But they that dared
Profane his kingly mantle won too well
Th' Assassin's guerdon, till the thoughts that dwell
In guilty bosoms deem'd the bloody shade
Of murder'd Cæsar stalk'd abroad, to tell
Rome's doom at Philippi!—Ah, *there* was play'd
A game whose stake was Empires, lost or madly made! (¹)

(¹) "*Brutus.* Speak to me, what thou art.
 Ghost. Thy evil spirit, Brutus.
 Bru.   Why com'st thou?
 Ghost. To tell thee thou shalt see me at Philippi.
 Bru. Well;
  Then I shall see thee again?
 Ghost.   Ay, at Philippi.   [Ghost *vanishes.*"
      [*Shakespeare's* "*Julius Cæsar:*" *Act IV; Scene III.*

𝕵ulius 𝕮æsar.

C ÆSAR, the great Usurper! and the first
   In Moderation, as in sov'reign Will!—
He, he *alone* could slake the burning thirst
Of vast Ambition at the vernal rill
Of Strength, unmix'd with Frenzy!—slew until
Rome's foes were vanquish'd, but by Envy's knell
His star was quench'd in darkness!—Lo! his skill
   Curs'd Mankind through example!—by the spell
Of his illusive glory, millions dared and fell!

𝕵𝖚𝖑𝖎𝖚𝖘 𝕮𝖆𝖘𝖆𝖗.

NOT all may follow where high Genius leads!—
But by a Cæsar may a World be won!—
'Tis but *one* World, *one* Cæsar, where such deeds
But by an equal Genius may be done!—
And who, of men, dare claim the Triple Sun
Which fix'd the first great Cæsar on Fame's
 throne?—
Historian! Prince! Debater! three in one!— (¹)
He stood, he stands, must *ever* stand alone!—
Creation, say! can'st boast his like since Time hath flown?

(¹) Modern History may boast such another triplicate character: I refer to Michael Angelo, who was a Sculptor, a Painter and a Poet — but not by any means in equal perfection, since his Poesy required the sunbeams of a late love to ripen it, and late fruit is seldom equal to that which buds earlier. To this trio of magnificent talents must be added that of a great Architect, as St. Peter's will attest to future generations.

𝕵𝖚𝖑𝖎𝖚𝖘 𝕮æ𝖘𝖆𝖗.

LAS, for human Justice! They that bear
The towering weight of Empire find their crown
Twined from the thorn-bush, and the ceaseless
    care,
That robs their days of Gladness, a renown
Dear-purchas'd with their breath! The king and
    clown
Oft fill a common grave! — together sleep
The sceptreless and sceptred! They whose frown
Awed trembling senates or bade millions weep,
Wrapt in the mould'ring shroud, "pale Hecate's" (¹)
    revel keep!

(¹)   — " now witchcraft celebrates
Pale Hecate's offerings ; " etc.
    [*Shakespeare's* " *Macbeth :* " *Act II ; Scene I.*

Mark Antony.

M ARK Antony! who rous'd the heart of Rome,
    And bade the "poor, dumb mouths" ([1]) of Cæsar
      speak
    Until each purple tear swell'd to a tome
    Of moving eloquence, whilst thy flush'd cheek,
    Curv'd lip and kindling eye, did threat'ning wreak
    Against his base subverters! Had'st thou been
    Impregnable to Pleasure, and a Greek, ([2])
    As in all else a *Roman*, thou wert kin
To Earth's great patriots, nor had stoop'd to Love's
      sweet sin!

([1]) *Shakespeare's "Julius Cæsar:" Act III; Scene II.*

([2]) The reference is more particularly to the Spartan Greeks, although the Athenians were considered to be equally brave.

CANTO I.

Mark Antony.

O H! why would'st thou, who might'st have been of
   men
A paragon and hero, thus descend
To Love's material pleasures? Wherefore, when
Fair Fortune smiled upon thee, would'st thou blend
The fleeting and eternal till the end
Shrank to Forgetfulness, and Egypt's Queen (¹)
Eclips'd thy Sun of Glory? Why pretend
Man of celestial nature? — wherefore screen,
With Sanctity, a thing whose joy hath been so mean?

(¹) " Oh! too convincing — dangerously dear —
In woman's eye, the unanswerable tear;
That weapon of her weakness she can wield,
To save, subdue — at once her spear and shield:
Avoid it — Virtue ebbs and Wisdom errs,
Too fondly gazing on that grief of hers!
What lost a world, and bade a hero fly?
The timid tear in Cleopatra's eye."
                   [*Byron's " Corsair:" Canto II.*

𝔓𝔞𝔰𝔰𝔦𝔬𝔫.

O, WOMAN! wherefore is't that thou wert made
At onceMan's crown and cursing? From the dust
Thy beauty hymns us, but, when once essay'd
Starr'd Heaven's inviting steep, the cank'ring rust
Of Blight and fleshly failing, Love's fair lust,
Hurls us from the far summit we aspire
Into a Cretan labyrinth where our trust
Grows weak and wav'ring, and Chimeras dire—
Minotaurs(¹) of the Mind, quench our immortal fire!

(¹) The Cretan Minotaur was "a monster with a bull's body and a human head.
It was exceedingly strong and fierce, and was kept in a labyrinth constructed by
Dædalus, so artfully contrived that whoever was enclosed in it could by no means
find his way out unassisted. Here the Minotaur roamed, and was fed with human victims."

[" *The Age of Fable;*" *Bulfinch.*

CANTO I.

𝕻𝖆𝖘𝖘𝖎𝖔𝖓.

THUS hath it ever been, and yet must be
Whilst Man, proud slave of Passion, plods below,
And deems himself an Angel whose haught (¹)knee
Stoops but to God!—methinks the soul-like (²) flow
Of Circumstance doth bend some mightier bow—
That Time's dread purpose marks a loftier aim
Than piping this lost Cherub, for we know
Not that which lies about us, yet I claim
Bright worlds of brighter Spirits feed the Poet's flame!

(¹) Haught—haughty. — "No lord of thine, thou *haught*, insulting man," etc.
    [*Shakespeare's* "*King Richard II:*" *Act IV; Scene I.*
    — " and then his courage *haught*
Desyrd of forreine foemen to be knowne," etc.
    [*Spenser's* "*Faerie Queene:*" *Book I; Canto VI.*
(²) "Ye pine groves, with your soft and *soul-like* sounds !"
[*Coleridge's* "*Hymn before Sunrise, in the Valley of Chamouni, Switzerland.*"

Augustus.

A UGUSTUS, haughty tyrant! Father! Foe!
Specious despoiler of the People's right!
  Thou sov'reign, proud, ambitious, who did'st sow
  At once the seed of Probity and Blight,
  Be thou remember'd as a dubious light—
  An *ignis-fatuus* that too brightly shone,
  And laps'd again to darkness; — Lo! the night
  Wax'd deeper with thy setting — thou alone
Could'st dazzle whilst thou wrong'd, nor tremble 'pon
    thy throne!

Augustus.

THY courts were those of Learning, where the Lyre
To Virgil, Horace, Ovid, Livy, sang
In grand, soul-stirring numbers whose deep fire
Enrich'd all-after time, for in them rang
The tones of Immortality, which sprang
To life through Exaltation or the pain
Of parted Love — a wild and with'ring pang
Which seals the Soul's clear fountain till the brain,
Lull'd to a pensive sadness, courts its cank'ring chain.

Augustus.

A UGUSTUS! 'pon thy scutcheon gleams the stain
Of Rome's thrice precious blood, great Cicero's:(¹)
Alas! that thou, who ever in the main
Sought Wisdom's councils, should'st provide thy
   foes
So dread and just a weapon to depose
Thee from Time's benefactors, or incur
A lasting blight upon thy star which rose
Amid Earth's brightest: why would'st thou prefer,
With Love at free command, thus thy dark Soul
   t' aver?

(¹) Although the life of Rome's great orator was sacrificed more immediately
to the hatred of Mark Antony, yet his death may be more justly attributed to
Augustus, the leading spirit of the second Triumvirate.

CANTO I.

ℜeligion.

RELIGION! purple crimes crouch at thy door,
  And mark thy march of Progress!—of their kind,
  For thee, Mankind grew haters, and the poor
  Were trampl'd by the potent, till the Mind,
  The bright "Promethean spark," (¹) groped with
    the blind
  In outer Darkness, and the starry beam
  Of Christ's profaned religion fail'd to find
  A native worshipper, till one might deem
The Cross, and Calv'ry's Mount, some dark, distorted
    dream!

(¹) *Byron's "Manfred:" Act I; Scene I.*

Arians and Gnostics.

THEN rose the Arian sect with bloody hand,
And smote the subtler Gnostic, till the tide
Whelm'd with a crimson deluge the lost land
In universal Slaughter, and the pride
Of ghostly fathers strove no more to hide
Their dark ambitions; ([1]) then the holy well
Of St. Theonas flow'd with gore that dyed
The pavement to the altar, where men fell,
A prayer upon their lips, and pass'd ([2]) without a
knell! ([3])

([1]) *See " Gibbon's Rome : " Vol. III; p. 376.*
([2]) *Tennyson's " Morte d'Arthur," or " Passing of Arthur."*
([3]) *See " Gibbon's Rome : " Vol. III; p. 379.*

CANTO I.

Athanasius.

YET *one* commands a high and holier place
  Amidst this wide sedition; let us pause
To honor Athanasius, ([1]) and embrace
Awhile a gentler prospect in this cause
Where mutual Hate voids Pity's milder laws,
And human creatures, in unnatural strife,
Pollute with blood Christ's Banner which ignores
The purple propagation of the knife,
Nor sanctifies the wretch who spills the meanest life!

([1]) *See " Gibbon's Rome : " Vol. III; p.* 356.

Plato--The Logos--The Triad.

O, PLATO! thou did'st shadow forth, of yore,
The mystic *Logos* of the Nicene creed! —
The awful Triad, at whose triple door
Wisdom   falls,   shatter'd,   like   the   storm-bent
    reed! — (¹)
What is this creature, Man, that he hath need
To beat his puny pinions 'gainst the bars
Of Earth's dim prison, till they droop and bleed?—
Methinks the wild-bird's instinct 'tis that jars
Against our slavish bonds, still pointing toward the
    stars!

(¹) *See* " *Gibbon's Rome:* " *Vol. III; p.* 314, 315, 320, 332.

𝔍𝔬𝔳𝔢 𝔞𝔫𝔡 𝔖𝔢𝔪𝔢𝔩𝔢.

I HOLD it be not we are thus abased
  Save through some purpose, yet this scathing
    flame,
  Be it for good or ill, seems interlaced
  In an unjust proportion with our frame;
  At least in Souls that tempt fair Semele's fame,
  By Jove consumed to ashes when he stood,
  In radiant panoply, before the dame,
  Soft partner of his love, whose lip had woo'd
The God's rash promise in his least ungentle mood.([1])

([1]) Semele, doubting if her lover were indeed immortal Jove, required from him the fulfillment of any desire she might express. Jupiter, though somewhat loth, consented. She then pronounced the words, which "The King of Gods and Men," bound by his fatal oath, could neither recall nor deny. "In deep distress he left her and returned to the upper regions. There he clothed himself in his

𝔓𝔞𝔰𝔰𝔦𝔬𝔫.

THUS hath it ever been with those who rend
   In twain the Web of Darkness, which is flung
'Twixt God and our dim natures that so blend
The earthly and angelic: thus we hung,
Pois'd 'mid immortal glories, till the tongue
Of the Arch-Tempter charm'd us to the brink
Of everlasting Ruin, where, among
Earth's host of prurient passions, still we drink
This Hemlock of the Mind, and more degraded sink!

---

splendors, not putting on all his terrors, as when he overthrew the giants, but
what is known among the Gods as his lesser panoply. Arrayed in this he entered
the chamber of Semele. Her mortal frame could not endure the splendors of the
immortal radiance. She was consumed to ashes."

[" *The Age of Fable;* " *Bulfinch.*

𝕿𝖍𝖊 𝕳𝖚𝖒𝖆𝖓 𝕸𝖎𝖓𝖉.

A LAS! that Man, " The noblest work of God,"(¹)
Endow'd with Mind, clear Reason's calm Sub-
lime, —
At whose disputeless and almighty nod
The Bolt outstrips the rushing Car of Time,
And bears his mandates on, from clime to clime,
'Neath frighted Neptune's privileged domain,
Where sea-calves gambol 'mid the dank caves'
slime, —
That Man, the demi-Angel, form'd to reign
O'er all created creatures — in whose godlike brain

(¹) *Pope's Essay on Man: " Epistle IV.*

The Human Mind.

THE Universe seems imaged — from the breast
  Of whose far-darting Ægis beams the might
Of Power supreme, like dread Medusa's crest
That deck'd the shield of Pallas, Goddess
    bright, — (¹)
Alas! this Emanation, splendour-dight
With arch-angelic glories, should decline
His mind to sensual Pleasure when his flight
Hymns with the star-eyed Cherubs, where "The
    Nine" (²)
Breathe o'er th' exalted Soul a spirit all divine!

(¹) The snaky head of the Gorgon, Medusa, having been severed from its body by the hero, Perseus, was affixed by Minerva to her shield.

(²) Muses.

CANTO I.

𝕵𝖚𝖑𝖎𝖆𝖓 𝖙𝖍𝖊 𝕬𝖕𝖔𝖘𝖙𝖆𝖙𝖊.

MARK now the great Apostate! he whose name
    Held a meridian glory, and display'd
The might of Rome's first Cæsar, dear to Fame!
Thrice did he dare what Cæsar *twice* essay'd!—
Thrice dared and triumph'd o'er a foe dismay'd!—
Thrice o'er the Rhine the Roman Eagles bore, (¹)
Ere hail'd "Augustus" (²) by each warrior's
    blade!—
Thrice "Came, and Saw, and Conquer'd," (³) as of
    yore   [deplore!
"The mightiest Julius," (⁴) whom true Wisdom must

(¹) *See " Gibbon's Rome : " Vol. III; p.* 228.
(²) *See " Gibbon's Rome : " Vol. IV; p.* 11.
(³) " Veni, Vidi, Vici." The motto inscribed upon the victorious banner of Julius Cæsar, and embodied in his letter to Rome.
(⁴) *Shakespeare's " Hamlet : " Act I; Scene I.*

𝕭ictories of 𝕵ulian.

T O Julian th' Alemanni suppliant bow'd—
   Surmar and Hortaire, chiefs of royal line;
'Pon Strasbourg's plain their kings and nobles
   proud
Met Fortune's ebbing flood, and saw decline
Chnodomar's star of Conquest and Rapine;
Then, 'gainst the Franks, turn'd Gaul's victorious
   arms —
Those fierce barbarians who would ne'er define
A law save "Die or Conquer!"— War's alarms
To their rude Souls seem'd music fraught with gentlest
   charms! ([1])

([1]) *See " Gibbon's Rome : " Vol. III; p.* **224, 225, 229.**

𝕻𝖎𝖈𝖙𝖔𝖗𝖎𝖊𝖘 𝖔𝖋 𝕵𝖚𝖑𝖎𝖆𝖓.

THE Eye of Night beheld the Rhine's broad stream
  Fleck'd with the Roman galleys, whose swift stroke
Sped armèd warriors, 'neath her silv'ry beam,
Upon the German camp; nor yet awoke
The drowsy sentinel till fiercely broke
The Foeman's vengeful shout, which fix'd his
  doom:
To arms! To arms! 'neath Darkness' sable cloak,
Gaul's hardy veterans people many a tomb
With an untimely shadow, in the midnight gloom! (¹)

(¹) *See " Gibbon's Rome :" Vol. III; p.* 229, 230.

𝕮ictories of 𝕵ulian.

HARK! Bacchus' rites are hush'd!—the thirsty brand
Drinks purple nectar from each flowing wound!—
The wine-cup trembles in the palsied hand,
And adds its ruby to the redd'ning ground,
All slippery with Slaughter! — far around,
The death-groan echoes to Love's deep farewell,
Where mingling prayers and curses loud resound,
Proclaiming to the Winds this work of Hell —
This glutless, tigerish thirst of fiends that in us dwell! (¹)

(¹) *See* " *Gibbon's Rome:* " *Vol. III; p.* 229, 230.

CANTO I.

Victories of Julian.

THE strife is o'er! — pale Cynthia's parting beam
Views many a lordly crest amid the slain,
Whose glittering helms glance, 'neath her fading
    gleam,
Like moon-kiss'd billows 'pon the dark-blue main;
Whilst many a blade, yet grasp'd in proud disdain,
Attests the vanquish'd hero's victory;
And Death, whose mantle shrouds the gory plain,
May boast no bloodless triumph! — here the free
Barbarian bravely fell, nor shrank from Fate's decree!

𝕵ulian 𝕻roclaimed 𝕰mperor.

VIEW now the scene of Gaul's gay Capital! —
A martial banquet spread — the ruddy wine
Fill'd to each beaker's brim!　Ere young Morn
　　shall
Dethrone pale Hesperus, the royal line
Of Europe's Conqueror, great Constantine,
Shall haste to setting! — Hark! borne from afar,
The swell of angry voices sounds decline
To that world-honor'd name! — The Julian star
Salutes, with modest pride, the Gallic host's huzza! (¹)

(¹) *See " Gibbon's Rome:"　Vol. IV; p.* 10, 11.

CANTO I.

𝔍𝔢𝔯𝔲𝔰𝔞𝔩𝔢𝔪.

A ND thine, Jerusalem's, thrice-holy Mounts! —
Sion and Acra's consecrated ground! —
Ye heard restor'd e'en here, where the first founts
Of Christ's Religion flow'd, that impious sound,
The Pagan's profanation! — ye saw crown'd,
By Venus' Temple, old Moriah's steep! —
Ye felt the ploughshare where no crops abound,
Save seed sown of the Shepherd that His sheep
May perish not unheeded where they will but reap! (¹)

(¹) *See " Gibbon's Rome : " Vol. IV; p.* 99, 100.

Rebuilding of the Temple.

THE Pagan's power declined! — his false fane fell ([1])
Before th' encroaching Christian — and again,
At a then distant day, *one* sought to swell
The joyful hope of Juda! — Who, 'mong men,
Was he? — The proud Apostate! — from Fear's fen
Plucking the pious Hebrew to rebuild
The temple to his God, till, wondrous, when
The silver pick was plied, Jehovah still'd
By the bright bolts of Heaven! — thus His Wrath's
    word fulfill'd!

([1]) *See " Gibbon's Rome:" Vol. IV; p.* 103, 104, 105, 106.

Grove and Temple of Daphne.

I N Daphne's laurell'd shrine the Sun God stood,
  Symmetric Beauty moulding each light limb,
Whilst, graceful stooping, he fair Tellus woo'd,
As stream'd Jove's nectar o'er the chalice' brim,
Staining his ivory palm, where the bright rim
Shower'd its purply vintage o'er the ground
In rich libations, till the Temple dim
Glow'd with celestial Splendour, whilst the sound
Of rapturous music rose, and ravish'd those around! ([1])

([1]) *See " Gibbon's Rome:" Vol. IV; p.* 118, 120.

Grove and Temple of Daphne.

SUCH was the scene of yore, yet, when there stood
   The Foe of Christ within that crumbling wall,
Its prescient pride was perish'd! — when he woo'd
Apollo at his shrine, through the stript hall
A hollow whisper but obey'd Hope's call! —
The throng of men and maids, in shrouds of snow,
Where, where are they? — Alas! full lightly fall
The Sun's beams 'bove this spot, though none shall
   know
All his bright Orb beheld of yon proud pageant's glow! ([1])

([1]) *See "Gibbon's Rome:" Vol. IV; p.* 120, 121.

𝕿𝖍𝖊 𝕻𝖆𝖑𝖆𝖙𝖎𝖓𝖊 𝕳𝖎𝖑𝖑.

PAUSE! for ye near the perish'd Palatine!
   Form'd yon gray, mould'ring turrets the abode
Of Rome's dread Majesty? — the dim decline
Of Age hath shorn their lustre, and the load
Of wasted centuries Time's seed hath sowed
In one wide desolation! Babylon,
The Royal Harlot, knew no harsher code
When stripp'd of her full greatness! If, anon,
The mighty dead could wake, where were thy glories
     gone?

𝕻alaces of the 𝕮æsars.

D UST of departed Greatness!   Here hath soar'd
Each Palace of the Cæsars, now no more! —
Wide-scatter'd wrecks of Ruin, which afford
Fit fund for Contemplation!   In the core
Of hearts such scenes grow hallow'd through the
      law
Of past Association, whilst the beam
Which bathed applausive millions, and of yore
Announc'd the Gods of Genius, like a dream
Thrills o'er each ravish'd sense with transitory gleam!

Charles Dickens.

WHILST wond'ringly we view yon hoary hill,
   Exemplar of the Past! list to a strain   [thrill
From one whose mute, hush'd harp no more may
With its once matchless music — a refrain
Of Albyn's peerless novelist! I drain
A cup to memory of him whose page
Imperishably stands, while men retain
The reverence due Genius, to engage
The Soul's sweet sympathies in scion as in sage! (¹)

(¹) My readers will, I am sure, pardon the liberty I have taken in introducing this exquisite gem as a note, and, the more readily, that the author of "Pickwick" has so seldom courted the Muse. Long may his noble words survive, to lighten the burdens and lessen the trials of humanity! —

     " Oh, a dainty plant is the Ivy green,
        That creepeth o'er ruins old!
     Of right choice food are his meals I ween,
        In his cell so lone and cold.

Triumphal Arches.

HERE press'd the pageantry of Rome's proud throng!

Through thrice an hundred Triumphs did'st thou glow,

Ye ivy-mantl'd Arches which belong,

Like things ye view'd, to centuries laid low

By Time, the Monarch's Monarch, and the foe

The wall must be crumbled, the stone decayed,
To pleasure his dainty whim:
And the mouldering dust that years have made
Is a merry meal for him.
Creeping where no life is seen,
A rare old plant is the Ivy green.

" Fast he stealeth on, though he wears no wings,
And a staunch old heart has he.
How closely he twineth, how tight he clings,
To his friend the huge Oak Tree!

CANTO I.

To Man's o'er-ripen'd Greatness!—Thou, O Fame!
Alone can'st grant his puny breath to blow
Pipes to succeeding millions, or a name
To kindle o'er his dust deep Mem'ry's deathless flame!

And slyly he traileth along the ground,
    And his leaves he gently waves,
As he joyously hugs and crawleth round
    The rich mould of dead men's graves.
        Creeping where grim Death has been,
        A rare old plant is the Ivy green.

" Whole Ages have fled and their works decayed,
    And Nations have scattered been;
But the stout old Ivy shall never fade,
    From its hale and hearty green.
The brave old plant in its lonely days,
    Shall fatten upon the Past:
For the stateliest building Man can raise
    Is the Ivy's food at last.
        Creeping on, where Time has been,
        A rare old plant is the Ivy green.''
                    [*Dickens' " Ivy Green."*

𝔉𝔬𝔯𝔲𝔪 𝔎𝔬𝔪𝔞𝔫𝔲𝔪.

W AS this the stately Forum?—This the place
     Of Temples and of Triumphs? Yes! despoil'd
Of Trophy, Arch, Urn, Column, still we trace
Strewn fragments of bright Beauty which have
     foil'd
The avarice of Age, though Blight hath soil'd
Their days of dewy Splendour—whilst the thought
Of mighty Cicero, each feud embroil'd
'Twixt the mad multitudes, beam phantoms
     wrought   [caught!
By Retrospection's wand, i' the Soul's spectrum (¹)

(¹) "The elongated figure, formed in a dark chamber, of the seven prismatic
colors, into which a beam of the Sun's light is decomposed, by admitting it
through an opening in the window-shutter, and letting it fall on a prism."

[*Olmsted.*

Fountains at Rome.

THE plash of lapsing waters, soft accord,
 Sweet Psalmody of Sound, floats on the air
With intermingling echoes! — th' halcyon sward
Bestrewn by sparkling dew-drops! — Naught of
 Care
Assails the wearied Mind! — here they that bear
May cast aside their burthens! — this is Rome!
The gush of myriad fountains breathes a prayer
Of native melody, whilst yon starr'd dome,
 The blue-arch'd vault of Heaven, spans Freedom's
 ancient home!

𝕹ight at 𝕽ome.

FOR such is Night beneath Italia's sky!
    The Summer Moon hath full'd, yet casts weird
       shades
    O'er this dispeopl'd spot! — the owlet's cry
    Re-echoes unreprov'd! — Remembrance fades
    Of this, our petty Present, and the blades
    Of heroes, here unsheath'd, recall each scene
    Of Pomp and martial Splendour! — cavalcades
    Of phantoms, and the fray, lit by the Queen
Of Darkness, pass me by with pale but lordly mien!

𝔏𝔬𝔯𝔡 𝔅𝔶𝔯𝔬𝔫 𝔙𝔦𝔫𝔡𝔦𝔠𝔞𝔱𝔢𝔡;

OR,

𝔅𝔬𝔪𝔢 𝔞𝔫𝔡 𝔥𝔢𝔯 𝔓𝔦𝔩𝔤𝔯𝔦𝔪.

CANTO THE SECOND.

"O, pardon me, thou piece of bleeding earth,
That I am meek and gentle with these butchers!
Thou art the ruins of the noblest man,
That ever livèd in the tide of times."

[*Shakespeare's* "*Julius Cæsar* :" *Act III*; *Scene I.*

Lord Byron Vindicated.

CANTO THE SECOND.

Coliseum. [1]

WE stand within the Coliseum's shade!
Oh, God! how grandly desolate! The stars
Above smile down like Angels that essay'd
To woo us to themselves! Here bloody Mars
Assembl'd his stern votaries in War's
Tumultuous conflict — Honour's, Pity's voice,
Nor Freedom's, nor the Right,the thirst debars
Of Murder's carnival, but all rejoice
To see the bright blood flow, applauding Fortune's
choice!

[1] The reader is requested to imagine him, or herself, beneath the tender

64

LORD BYRON VINDICATED;

CANTO II.

Coliseum.

A ND here fought famish'd beasts with fiercer men,
And Life hung in the balance whilst the press
Sate mute and breathless, as from out his den
The Nemean lion sprang! No faint distress
Unnerves his practis'd arm which might confess
The *Bestiarius'* (¹) fear, as, face to face,
The tawny monster stands! — One *passus* (²) less
And they must meet! — but see! the transient trace
Of Recollection fades — Defiance takes its place!

---

glories of an Italian Summer's night, as straying within the shadows of this, the
most sublime and awe-inspiring relic of the mighty Past, whilst before the
absorbed and dreamy vision pass — like King Richard's pale, midnight visitants —
the shades of the long-silent actors of this once so busy scene.

" — upon such a night
I stood within the Coliseum's wall,
[*Continued on next page.*]

(¹) The *Bestiarii* were men employed to combat with wild beasts in the arena.
(²) Pace.

CANTO II.

Coliseum.

W HY doth he seek with his sole arm to brave
The King of Beasts and Terrors? Know ye not
This man is but a bondsman — a vile slave —
The instrument of Passion — that his lot
Hath been but stripes and lashes?— hast forgot
He wooes a manlier death where Courage calls?
Ha! Look! the huge cat springs!—A gleam is
shot —
The glint of glittering steel!—One vast paw falls,
Shattering the slight skull — the Soul's puissant walls!

Midst the chief relics of almighty Rome ;
The trees which grew along the broken arches
Waved dark in the blue midnight, and the stars
Shone through the rents of ruin ; from afar
The watch-dog bay'd beyond the Tiber ; and
More near from out the Cæsars' palace came
The owl's long cry, and, interruptedly,
Of distant sentinels the fitful song

𝕮oliseum.

C AN these be *men* that joy in human pain?
  Ay! Men and Romans! — Rulers of the Earth!
But dies he unaveng'd?   No! they were twain
In Slavery as Death — a common hearth
Had bred this lowly pair that from their birth
Had shared the same harsh fate; and now he hastes,
This brother helot, to avenge the worth
Of his slain comrade where the flush'd fiend tastes
His warm and fragrant blood which o'er the Circus
    wastes!

Begun and died upon the gentle wind.
Some cypresses beyond the time-worn beach
Appeared to skirt the horizon, yet they stood
Within a bow-shot. — Where the Cæsars dwelt,
And dwell the tuneless birds of night, amidst
A grove which springs through levell'd battlements,
And twines its roots with the imperial hearths,
Ivy usurps the laurel's place of growth; —

CANTO II.

Coliseum.

'TWERE rash to face him now! The red lips reek
With Life's yet thermal tide, and that fierce thirst
Which slumber'd in his veins now bids him seek,
Not shun, this fresh affray! Few, few had durst
Provoke the savage ire, by Famine nurst,
Wherewith he turns to front his wary foe! —
Aloft the bright blade gleams! — One mighty burst
Of Rage and mad Despair — one final throe,
And stretch'd along the dust the baffl'd brute lies low!

But the gladiators' bloody Circus stands,
A noble wreck in ruinous perfection!
While Cæsar's chambers and the Augustan halls,
Grovel on earth in indistinct decay. —
And thou didst shine, thou rolling moon, upon
All this, and cast a wide and tender light,
Which soften'd down the hoar austerity
Of rugged desolation, and fill'd up,

𝕮oliseum.

ENOUGH of Crime and Carnage!   It were fit
The scene were shrouded here, but o'er our view
Expands a bloodier prospect as there flit,
Beneath the mantling moon-beams, which imbue
The place with their pale aspect and wan hue,
The shades of those who fell for the mad sport
Of the rude populace — that Cain-mark'd crew,
The Gladiators' band — those fiends who fought
To glut the wolfish thirst which Mercy set at naught!

As 't were anew, the gaps of centuries;
Leaving that beautiful which still was so,
And making that which was not, till the place
Became religion, and the heart ran o'er
With silent worship of the great of old! —
The dead, but sceptered sovereigns, who still rule
Our spirits from their urns. — "
          [*Byron's "Manfred:" Act III; Scene IV.*

CANTO II.

(¹) **Coliseum.** (²)

A GAIN the lists grow peopled as we mark
The brawny Champions of the gory Ring—
Those madmen of a moment who embark
Their all in this frail venture which may bring
But Death—perchance Dishonor: yet they fling
Away their lives like baubles, to embrace
A mute, inglorious fate, or win a thing
As trivial as the Wind—the sorry grace   [efface!
That dwells in fleeting breath, which Chance may soon

(¹) Longfellow thus alludes to the fennel, and the *fennel-wreath* with which a victorious gladiator was crowned:—

> "It gave new strength, and fearless mood;
> And gladiators, fierce and rude,
> Mingled it in their daily food;
> And he who battled and subdued,
> A *wreath of fennel* wore."
>   [*Longfellow's* " *Goblet of Life.*"

(²) "Type of the antique Rome! Rich reliquary
Of lofty contemplation left to Time
By buried centuries of pomp and power!

[*Continued on next page.*]

𝕮𝖔𝖑𝖎𝖘𝖊𝖚𝖒.

I SEE the gaping wound — the bloody dews
That dye his feeble brow — the quivering limb,
Convuls'd — or the fine agony which wooes
The gentle Drops of Pity, cherubim
That veil bright Orbs of Beauty, which o'er-brim
Fond Nature's genial founts!   The glazing eye
Turns with expiring glance, tender but dim,
Toward his far home, and, as he sinks, a sigh
Betrays unto the jeering horde his heart's blest tie! —

    *   *   *   *   *

Here, where a hero fell, a column falls!
Here, where the mimic eagle glared in gold,
A midnight vigil holds the swarthy bat!
Here, where the dames of Rome their gilded hair
Waved to the wind, now wave the reed and thistle!
Here, where on golden throne the monarch lolled,
Glides, spectre-like, unto his marble home,
Lit by the wan light of the hornéd moon,
The swift and silent lizard of the stones!

    *   *   *   *   *

CANTO II.

𝕮oliseum.

A ND now 'tis past. Now once again I hear
A last appeal for Mercy, where, o'ercome,·
A vanquish'd hero craves the general ear
To spare his forfeit life; —Yea! *hear!*—the dumb,
Pain'd gesture quells the low but eager hum
Of the hush'd throng, as all its vast array
Proclaims the People's sentence!—the fell thumb,(¹)
Uplifted, seals his doom! —Swift to obey,
Descends the brutal blow which terminates the fray!

These stones — alas! these gray stones — are they all —
All of the famed, and the colossal left
By the corrosive Hours to Fate and me?

'Not all' — the Echoes answer me — 'not all!

(¹) A Gladiator, vanquished in the sports of the Amphitheatre, had the privilege of a last appeal for life to the clemency of the audience. The decision of the people was signified by the dipt or uplifted thumb; the former granting pardon — the latter sealing his doom.

Coliseum.

SUCH still the scene where the wild wall-flower
    waves,
Garlanding the "blue midnight" (¹) with its wreath
Wove from the mould of Empires, o'er the graves
Of all Man deem'd eternal — he whose breath
Seem'd scarce less fleeting: Lo! we pause beneath
Thy gray, dismantl'd ruin, to accord
Our minds with the dim distance in this dearth
Of wondrous things that were, and say, " O, Lord!
Behold our works and Thine! — which must Mankind
    applaud?"

Prophetic sounds and loud, arise forever
From us, and from all Ruin, unto the wise,
As melody from Memnon to the Sun.'"
                              [*Poe's " Coliseum."*

(¹) *Byron's " Manfred:" Act III; Scene IV.*

Coliseum.

H ERE star-eyed Flora spreads her fairy sway,
With score-score children scatter'd wide around, (¹)
Embowering by green garlands grim Decay,
And thickly trailing o'er each grass-grown mound;
Whilst from the time-worn parapet, embrown'd,
Depends each weird festoon's fantastic wave,
Coquetting with the moon-beam which hath found
In these, her gentler playmates, forms that gave
To Fame a Byron's page (²) which breathes beyond the
Grave! — (³)

(¹) The Coliseum has been found to contain no less than *four hundred and
twenty* different varieties of flora.

(²) " The first and second cantos of ' Childe Harold's Pilgrimage ' produced, on
their appearance in 1812, an effect upon the public, at least equal to any work which
[*Continued on page 78.*]

(³) " You may break, you may shatter the vase, if you will,
But the scent of the roses will hang round it still."
[*Moore's " Irish Melodies."*

𝔉𝔞𝔪𝔢.

O, CHRIST! the cost of such! Our sunny Youth
Consum'd 'mid self-sought tortures! — the worn
    breast
Wrung by forbidden searchings after Truth
That ever courts, but all eludes, our quest! —
Oh! to what end woo we this wild unrest —
The scathèd Spirit and the burning Brain? (¹)
Despair may seek to free the star-born Guest,
But, if fond Faith forbid us rend the chain, [pain! (²)
We writhe through wretched years of more than mortal

(¹) " Sit, Jessica : look, how the floor of heaven
    Is thick inlaid with patines of bright gold :
    There's not the smallest orb which thou behold'st,
    But in his motion like an angel sings,
    Still quiring to the young-ey'd cherubins, —

(²) " Truth for ever on the scaffold, Wrong for ever on the throne, — " etc.
                              [*Lowell's " Present Crisis."*

CANTO II.

ℑame.

V AIN Hope! to deem this bitter breath we draw
Abundant offering to thankless Time—
Or think her minions reverence, the more,
Sweet harps which swell with strains of idle rhyme
Earth's empty plaint—that from the Soul's fair
    clime
Deaf ears drink such sad sounds!—Serenely won
The Spirit's shining shore, methinks the chime
Of yon soft-choiring Spheres should suffer none
Save Seraphs' songs to swell, supreme, beyond the
    Sun! (¹)

Such harmony is in immortal souls;
But whilst this muddy vesture of decay
Doth grossly close us in, we cannot hear it."
    [*Shakespeare's "Merchant of Venice:" Act V; Scene I.*

(¹) [M. S. " Save seraphs' songs to swell sweet psalms beyond the Sun." — E.]

Fame.

YE who peruse the Poet's pensive page
    Full little ken those pangs that pour'd it forth,
Else should sad sympathies your Souls engage —
True tears attest glad Gratitude's blest birth: (¹)
With our hearts' blood we write!   Ah! little worth
His fyttes (²) that from fair founts of Joyaunce
    flow; —
The Prophet plods in pain the paths of Earth,
Where Sorrow soothes the Eloquence of Woe, (³)
For Pleasaunce featly (⁴) flies it is pursued the moe! (⁵)

(¹) "Not from a vain or shallow thought
      His awful Jove young Phidias brought."
                              [*Emerson's " Problem."*
(²) Strains.
(³) "No words suffice the secret soul to show,
      For Truth denies all eloquence to Woe."
                              [*Byron's " Corsair : " Canto III.*
(⁴) Nimbly.   (⁵) More.

CANTO II.

𝕱𝖆𝖒𝖊.

WITH our hearts' blood we write! (^{1}) Could ye who trace,
How heedlessly, stern strivings of the Soul
Which would repose her from Fame's weary race —
Turn her tired steps toward Good's still grateful goal, —
Could ye view this — could ye divine the whole —
Yea! track the Spirit to her secret cell,
Ye would ne (^{2}) wonder that the ripe years roll,
Draped with bleak Barrenness, o'er those that dwell
From fellow-worms apart, nor hive with Earth's wide hell!

(^{1})   " Most wretched men
Are cradled into poetry by wrong:
They learn in suffering what they teach in song."
            [*Shelley's " Julian and Maddalo."*

(^{2}) Not.

𝔏𝔬𝔳𝔢.

POOR Fool! prat'st thou of Love?—hath Heaven
 indeed
Vouchsaf'd no worthier worship, that ye take
Creatures of clay to crown your trivial creed?
Why at such rills would ye your thirstings slake,
When rivers, rolling by, spread their bright lake
Of rare-reflected Beauty round your feet?
Yet Love, too, hath her minions who would wake
Harmonious whispers with their hot hearts' beat—
Lured by the Little God, they find such fetters sweet!

---

has appeared within this or the last century, and placed at once upon Lord Byron's head the garland for which other men of genius have toiled long, and which they have gained late. He was placed pre-eminent among the literary men of his country by general acclamation. It was amidst such feelings of admiration that he entered the public stage. Everything in his manner, person, and conversation, tended to maintain the charm which his genius had flung around him; and those admitted to his conversation, far from finding that the inspired poet sunk into ordinary mortality, felt themselves attached to him, not only by many noble qualities,

CANTO II.

𝕷𝖔𝖛𝖊.

FOND Love hath her frail legions! for the Tomb
Teems with pale populace which, drooping, died,
Slain by some sightless wound; but direr doom
Is theirs, worn wand'rers, fickle Fate denied
The Crypt's calm consolation! — these abide,
'Mid men, like living shadows, silently
Plodding Wreck's scowling path with sullen
    pride,
Hugging Bond's hateful chain whose clank will
    be
Hoar holocaust of hopes which won whilst fancy-free!

---

but by the interest of a mysterious, undefined, and almost painful curiosity. A countenance exquisitely modelled to the expression of feeling and passion, and exhibiting the remarkable contrast of very dark hair and eyebrows, with light and expressive eyes, presented to the physiognomist the most interesting subject for the exercise of his art. The predominating expression was that of deep and habitual thought, which gave way to the most rapid play of features when he

𝕷𝖔𝖛𝖊.

TIME scars stern tablets!—scores the blooming brow!
Darkly our days are number'd!   Age may set
Pain's seal 'pon sunny Youth!—yea! Sorrow plough
Deep furrows of four-score dread annals yet (¹)
Down clothe the cherub cheek! — Alas! the debt
Bequeath'd by our prime parents, through their
    shame,
Rests unrequited! —well doth Passion whet
The lip of lewd Desire that knights its name —
Coins Love for conynge (²) Lust, twin terms of Folly's
    flame!

---

engaged in interesting discussion; so that a brother poet compared them to the
sculpture of a beautiful alabaster vase, only seen to perfection when lighted up
from within.   The flashes of mirth, gaiety, indignation, or satirical dislike, which
frequently animated Lord Byron's countenance, might, during an evening's con-

---

(¹) Ere yet.   (²) Cunning.

CANTO II.

Love.

WHY, from the mystic Mind's immortal realm,
Must we resume frail fetters, forg'd below?
As Palinurus perish'd at his helm, (¹)
We, baffl'd, die by some defenceless blow,
When Pleasure waves her wand of Lethæan dew,

---

versation, be mistaken, by a stranger, for a habitual expression, so easily and so
happily was it formed for them all; but those who had an opportunity of studying
his features for a length of time, and upon various occasions, both of rest and
emotion, will agree that their proper language was that of melancholy. Sometimes shades of this gloom interrupted even his gayest and most happy moments."

[*Sir Walter Scott.*]

(¹) "Venus now interceded with Neptune to allow her son at last to attain the
wished-for goal and find an end to his perils on the deep. Neptune consented,
stipulating only for one life as a ransom for the rest. The victim was Palinurus,
the pilot. As he sat watching the stars, with his hand on the helm, Somnus sent
by Neptune approached in the guise of Phœbus and said, 'Palinurus, the breeze
is fair, the water smooth, and the ship sails steadily on her course. Lie down
awhile and take needful rest. I will stand at the helm in your place.' Palinurus
replied, 'Tell me not of smooth seas or favoring winds, — me who have seen so
much of their treachery. Shall I trust Æneas to the chances of the weather and

CANTO II.

Where Woman, with her wiles, perverts the
heart: —
In vain doth downy velvet veil from view
The tiger's trenchant terrors, but the dart
Of *Cupid's* cureless woundings deals a deadlier smart!

---

the winds? And he continued to grasp the helm and to keep his eyes fixed on
the stars. But Somnus waved over him a branch moistened with Lethæn dew, and
his eyes closed in spite of all his efforts. Then Somnus pushed him overboard
and he fell; but keeping his hold upon the helm, it came away with him. Neptune
was mindful of his promise and kept the ship on her track without helm or pilot,
till Æneas discovered his loss, and, sorrowing deeply for his faithful steersman
took charge of the ship himself.

There is a beautiful allusion to the story of Palinurus in Scott's 'Marmion,'
introduction to Canto I."

["*The Age of Fable;*" *Bulfinch.*

CANTO II.

𝔏𝔬𝔳𝔢.

FAIR Woman! thou wert framed a tender thing—
Th' avow'd adornment of voluptuous Ease!
When thy fond failings would presume to fling
O'er stern Ambition's path such snares as seize
Our minds' unguarded moments, till we leese (¹)
Sight of God's stars above us, worshipping
At clay-created altars, must our knees
Seek purer shrines—Song's Pegasean Spring— (²)
Cursing, as I do now, dread Circe's chambering!

(¹) Lose.
(²) *Milton's " Paradise Lost : " Book VII.*

𝕷𝖔𝖛𝖊.

G AZE on God's sky! Go seek His mighty main!
  These to Affection are rich recompense!
Mark yon bald mountain beetling 'bove the plain!
Such scenes inspire the Spirit with stern sense
Of Nature's naked grandeur — grown intense
We prize each purer part! Is this not more
Than dark'ning our wrought Souls with shadows
  dense —
Torn thunder-clouds of Passion whose swoln store
Hangs bursting 'bove our heads, or whelms with ruth-
  less roar? (¹)

(¹) "How beautiful this night! the balmiest sigh
  Which vernal Zephyrs breathe in Evening's ear
  Were discord to the speaking quietude

CANTO II.

Night Thoughts.

BLEST beam those thoughts, charm'd Night! that
thou can'st bring
Unto chaste Sorrow's children who explore
Thy shining secrets 'pon the pensive wing
Of musing Meditation: (¹) from the shore
Of Time's tomb'd Ocean swells a solemn roar,
Droning of dead Eternities which grow
Gigantic on our sense — god-like we soar
Beyond Earth's blind existence: years ago
My Youth woke such a strain — list to its whilom flow!

That wraps this moveless scene. Heaven's ebon vault,
Studded with stars unutterably bright,
Through which the moon's unclouded grandeur rolls,
Seems like a canopy which Love has spread
To curtain her sleeping world."

[*Shelley's " Queen Mab."*

(¹) "Live not the stars and mountains? Are the waves
Without a spirit?"

[*Byron's " Island:" Canto II.*

The Poet's Prayer.

LMIGHTY Father!
A Lo, my Soul doth speak!—
A deep Voice soundeth
Which will not be still!
Father! what am I?
Give some sign
In this vast silence—
Be I worm, or God?
All my full Soul
Doth open to Thee,
Mighty King!
Oh, but one whisper—
One faint gleam

To light my way!
Alone, I tread the path
Unto Thy throne,
Thy throne — my home!
Friends have I none
Save Thine eternal stars;
In agony, to them
I lift mine arms,
And oft they answer,
For, gazing on them,
The deep Voice is still!
To me Time hath no measure;
For in the realms of Thought
Brief days are cycles,
And the Winter's snow
Oft blasts the buds of Spring,

And Age and Youth makes one!—
Yet hail! bright realms of Thought!
Thou art the Poet's clime!
In thee there is no trace
Of dull Decay!
Born of the Soul,
Immortal Youth is thine!
From thy fair circle
No dear friends depart!
The *Poet's.* friends are flowers,
And unto *him* they speak
Of Heaven, and far glories
Bright as themselves!
Oft, when the heart grows still,
And dark'ning shadows fall
Athwart the dim path

That we tread in trust,
We spy some gentle flower
With blue eye turn'd toward Heaven,
And lo! a voiceless prayer
Ascendeth 'mid the perfume
Of its praise!
Sweet flower! thou hast not
Spent thy heart in vain,
For thy pure prayer
Hath touch'd a silver chord
Within my breast
Of harmony divine:
Have peace, proud Voice within! —
This flower hath spoke
More wisdom than the lips
Of scepter'd Kings!

𝔅𝔶𝔯𝔬𝔫.

I RANGE from my fit theme. Thus I resume
The thread that leads through the long labyrinth
My failing feet must tread, till, from the Tomb,
I mount to Immortality, passing the plinth
Of Death's dim portal, like pale Hyacinth, (¹)

(¹) The boy Hyacinthus, Apollo's favorite, was one day engaged with him at
a game of quoits. "Apollo, heaving aloft the discus, with strength mingled with
skill, sent it high and far. Hyacinthus watched it as it flew, and excited with the
sport ran forward to seize it, eager to make his throw, when the quoit bounded
from the earth and struck him in the forehead. He fainted and fell. The God,
as pale as himself, raised him and tried all his art to stanch the wound and retain the flitting life, but all in vain; the hurt was past the power of medicine. As
when one has broken the stem of a lily in the garden it hangs its head and turns
its flowers to earth, so the head of the dying boy, as if too heavy for his neck,
fell over on his shoulder. 'Thou diest, Hyacinth,' so spoke Phœbus, 'robbed of
thy youth by me. Thine is the suffering, mine the crime. Would that I could
die for thee ! But since that may not be, thou shalt live with me in memory and
in song. My lyre shall celebrate thee, my song shall tell thy fate, and thou shalt

CANTO II.

Fair flower besprent with blood. Boldly I weave
My summ'd Wrath's song, which many a museful
    month
Hath been my sole, sweet solace; but I grieve
Less for *myself,* than *one* whose wrongs I would
    retrieve! ([1])

become a flower inscribed with my regrets.' While Apollo spoke, behold the
blood which had flowed on the ground and stained the herbage, ceased to be
blood; but a flower of hue more beautiful than the Tyrian sprang up, resembling
the lily, if it were not that this is purple and silvery white. And this was not
enough for Phœbus; but to confer still greater honor, he marked the petals with
his sorrow and inscribed 'Ah! ah!' upon them, as we see to this day. The
flower bears the name of Hyacinthus, and with every returning spring revives
the memory of his fate. It was said that Zephyrus, (the West-wind), who was
also fond of Hyacinthus and jealous of his preference of Apollo, blew the quoit
out of its course to make it strike Hyacinthus."

                    [" *The Age of Fable;*" *Bulfinch.*
             — "pitying the sad death
      Of Hyacinthus, when the cruel breath
      Of Zephyr slew him; Zephyr penitent,
      Who now ere Phœbus mounts the firmament,
      Fondles the flower amid the sobbing rain."
                [*Keats's* "*Endymion:*" *Book I.*

([1]) "The sentiment of justice is so natural, so universally acquired by all mankind, that it seems to me independent of all law, all party, all religion."
                                    [*Voltaire.*

𝕭𝖞𝖗𝖔𝖓.

YEA! one hath stood amid this Wreck of Time,
"A ruin amidst ruins," (¹) for he came,
A lonely wand'rer, from his own bleak clime—
A Land he might have loved, but that her shame
Had shut him from her till the very name
Did breathe but Desolation, and he strove
To still his bosom's pleadings with a fame
World-wide and grand, which in its tissue wove
All that Ambition craved, denying naught save Love !(²)

(¹) *Byron's Childe Harold:" Canto IV; Stanza XXV.*

(²)   There are some by nature proud,
Who, patient in all else, demand but this—
To love and be beloved with gentleness:
And, being scorned, what wonder if they die
Some living death? This is not destiny,
But man's own wilful ill."
                [*Shelley's " Julian and Maddalo."*

" His Poetry can only perish with the English Language."
                [*Macaulay.*

CANTO II.

𝔅𝔶𝔯𝔬𝔫.

COMPANIONS of his Spirit! Prophets! Ye
Lone walls that look'd on Rome's meridian blaze!
How did he love, 'mid thy dim shades, to be
Resolv'd to Contemplation whilst Earth's days
Shrank to Forgetfulness, as the soft rays
Of Summer moonlight chequer'd where they fell
O'er Arch and ivied Column, till the Fays —
Those tiny sprites that populate the dell,
Crept forth from leafy caves to chant their midnight
spell! (¹)

(¹) I deem no apology is required for the introduction here of the following
exquisite and touching tribute, paid by one of England's most polished Poets to
the memory of an illustrious brother : —

" To the gate they came ;
And, ere the man had half his story done,
Mine host received the Master — one long used

𝕭𝖞𝖗𝖔𝖓.

THERE breathes a peace through that blest pause
    from strife —
The calm, deep midnight, when the soft stars glow
With milder radiance, and some loftier life
Thrills all our Being, pleading, sweet and low,

To sojourn among strangers, every where
(Go where he would, along the wildest track)
Flinging a charm that shall not soon be lost,
And leaving footsteps to be traced by those
Who love the haunts of Genius; one who saw,
Observed, nor shunned the busy scenes of life,
But mingled not, and mid the din, the stir,
Lived as a separate Spirit.
        Much had passed
Since last we parted; and those five short years —
Much had they told! His clustering locks were turned
Grey; nor did aught recall the Youth that swam
From Sestos to Abydos. Yet his voice,
Still it was sweet; still from his eye the thought
Flashed lightning-like, nor lingered on the way,

CANTO II.

For these immortal natures, whilst the throe
Of an awak'd Intelligence withdraws
Our Souls from this seal'd Lazar-house of Woe
Wherein we faintly languish: — Man adores, —
Ay! *What?* — Is it Earth's lusts, or the eternal Cause?

Waiting for words. Far, far into the night
We sat, conversing — no unwelcome hour,
The hour we met; and, when Aurora rose,
Rising, we climbed the rugged Apennine.   *   *   *   *
     *   *   *   *   He is now at rest;
And praise and blame fall on his ear alike,
Now dull in death. Yes, Byron, thou art gone,
Gone like a star that through the firmament
Shot and was lost, in its eccentric course
Dazzling, perplexing. Yet thy heart, methinks,
Was generous, noble — noble in its scorn
Of all things low or little; nothing there
Sordid or servile. If imagined wrongs
Pursued thee, urging thee sometimes to do
Things long regretted, oft, as many know,
None more than I, thy gratitude would build
On slight foundations: and, if in thy life

𝕭𝖞𝖗𝖔𝖓.

I LOVED him from my Childhood; of charm'd
Youth

He was the cherish'd idol that, with years,

Assumed the manlier likeness of a truth

Which woo'd and won my heart! What now

appears

Not happy, in thy death thou surely wert,
Thy wish accomplished; dying in the land
Where thy young mind had caught ethereal fire,
Dying in GREECE, and in a cause so glorious!
    They in thy train — ah, little did they think,
As round we went, that they so soon should sit
Mourning beside thee, while a Nation mourned,
Changing her festal for her funeral song;
That they so soon should hear the minute-gun,
As morning gleamed on what remained of thee,
Roll o'er the sea, the mountains, numbering
Thy years of joy and sorrow.

CANTO II.

A destiny, seem'd then, to my quick fears,
A mocking phantom which beguiled the sense
With dreams of young Ambition that my tears
Implor'd to stay!—Thank God! 'twas *no* pretense!—
Each day it fonder grew—my lone lot's recompense!

Thou art gone;
And he who would assail thee in thy grave,
Oh, let him pause! (¹) For who among us all,
Tried as thou wert—even from thine earliest years, —
When wandering, yet unspoilt, a highland-boy—
Tried as thou wert, and with thy soul of flame;
Pleasure, while yet the down was on thy cheek,
Uplifting, pressing, and to lips like thine,
Her charmèd cup—ah, who among us all
Could say he had not erred as much, and more?"
                  [*Rogers's " Italy : " Part I; Section XIX*

    (¹) "Such graves as his are pilgrim-shrines,
        Shrines to no code or creed confined, —
        The Delphian vales, the Palestines,
        The Meccas of the mind."
            [*Halleck's " Burns."*

𝔅𝔶𝔯𝔬𝔫.

A ND now, in Manhood's prime, I joy to feel
   Deep yearnings stir within me to fulfill
   Those boyish aspirations: (¹) there doth steal
   At times upon my Spirit the blest will
   Of such exalted Essences, until
   Forth from my brain a martial Pallas springs, (²)
   Arm'd *cap-à-pie*, to aid my virgin skill;
   And, spreading to the blast her eager wings,
Aloft my glad Soul soars where the blithe sky-lark
   sings! (³)

(¹) "The Child is father of the Man;" etc.

[*Wordsworth's* " *My Heart Leaps Up.*"

(²) "Minerva, (Pallas, Athene,) the goddess of wisdom, was the offspring of Jupiter, without a mother. She sprang forth from his head, completely armed."

[" *The Age of Fable ;*" *Bulfinch.*

(³) "But chief, the sky-lark warbles high
   His trembling thrilling extasy;
   And, lessening from the dazzled sight,
   Melts into air and liquid light."

[*Gray's* " *Posthumous Odes.*"

CANTO II.

𝔅𝔶𝔯𝔬𝔫.

A FLOOD of melting memories doth swell
Upon my tide of Being with the thought
Of him I love so tenderly and well; (¹)
Yet they who love, *avenge!* (²) I have not sought
This stern and bitter conflict — there is naught
I find to prize in Strife; but did I hear,
Unmov'd, dark doubtings which the quick (³) have
      wrought
   Around the now defenceless, I should fear
To stand before my God, so base must I appear!

(¹)   " — No pulse in my ambition
   Whose beatings were not measured from thy heart! "
            [*Bulwer's* " *Richelieu :* " *Act II ; Scene II.*
      (²) " And I, alas! too late to save !
       Yet all I then could give, I gave,
       'Twas some relief, our foe a grave."
                [*Byron's* " *Giaour.*"
(³) Quick — living. — " Now pile your dust upon the *quick* and dead," etc.
         [*Shakespeare's* " *Hamlet :* " *Act V ; Scene I.*

𝔅𝔶𝔯𝔬𝔫.

"AM I my brother's keeper?" could I say? (¹)
Am I my brother's keeper?   Yea, am I!
Dark Sleuths of Malice! ye must meet at bay
Him ye have hounded, for your wolfish cry
Hath rous'd a tardy Justice! — I deny
Coarse accusations such warp'd Souls have bred,
Casting a cunning net where the foul Lie(²)
Assumes a Seraph's aspect! — Ye have plead,
Unanswer'd, your fell cause — *I* vindicate the dead!(³)

(¹) "And the Lord said unto Cain, where is Abel thy brother?   And he said,
I know not: *Am I my brother's keeper!*"   [*Genesis: Chap. IV; v. 9.*

(²) I wish it distinctly understood that these epithets are in nowise applied to
the authoress of "*Uncle Tom's Cabin.*"

(³)   "You have deeply ventured;
      But all must do so who would greatly win:" etc.
            [*Byron's " Marino Faliero :" Act I; Scene II.*

CANTO II.

𝕭𝖞𝖗𝖔𝖓.

G ENTLE Patroclus! when triumphant Troy
Rejoic'd that thy bright prototype might wield
No more the gory falchion, what alloy
Of Prudence stay'd his speed as o'er the field
Flash'd great Achilles' car? (¹)   Shall I not shield

(¹) "Thus far Patroclus had succeeded to his utmost wish in repelling the Tro-
jans and relieving his countrymen, but now came a change of fortune. Hector,
borne in his chariot, confronted him. Patroclus threw a vast stone at Hector, which
missed its aim, but smote Cebriones, the charioteer, and knocked him from the
car. Hector leaped from the chariot to rescue his friend, and Patroclus also de-
scended to complete his victory. Thus the two heroes met face to face. At this
decisive moment the poet, as if reluctant to give Hector the victory, records that
Phœbus took part against Patroclus. He struck the helmet from his head and
the lance from his hand. At the same moment *an obscure Trojan wounded him
in the back,* and Hector, pressing forward, pierced him with his spear. He fell,
mortally wounded. Then arose a tremendous conflict for the body of Patroclus;
but his armor was at once taken possession of by Hector, who, retiring a short distance, divested himself of his own armor and put on that of Achilles, then returned

CANTO II.

Thee, too, *my* wrong'd Patroclus? — Ay! Truth's
sake (¹)   [hath steel'd
Gird me with God's great might? Thy cause
Mine arm with mail of proof, the which shall make
Me equal to my task, nor threats my purpose shake!

---

to the fight. * * * * Then Achilles went forth to battle inspired with a rage
and thirst for vengeance that made him irresistible. * * * * Achilles secured
behind his shield waited the approach of Hector. When he came within reach
of his spear, Achilles choosing with his eye a vulnerable part where the armor
leaves the neck uncovered, aimed his spear at that part, and Hector fell, death-
wounded, and feebly said, 'Spare my body! Let my parents ransom it, and let
me receive funeral rites from the sons and daughters of Troy.' To which Achilles replied, 'Dog, name not ransom nor pity to me, on whom you have brought
such dire distress. No! trust me, nought shall save thy carcass from the dogs.
Though twenty ransoms and thy weight in gold were offered, I would refuse it
all.' So saying he stripped the body of its armor, and fastening cords to the
feet tied them behind his chariot, leaving the body to trail along the ground. Then
mounting the chariot he lashed the steeds and so dragged the body to and fro
before the city."   ["*The Age of Fable;*" *Bulfinch.*

(¹) " Truth crushed to earth shall rise again :
     The eternal years of God are hers ;
     But Error, wounded, writhes with pain,
     And dies among his worshippers."
                    [*Bryant's* " *Battle-field.*"

CÀNTO II.

𝕭𝖞𝖗𝖔𝖓.

I QUESTION not the cold, (¹) though some have
been
The Grave should not have shielded — these shall
sleep! —
Their Souls now stand to answer each past sin
Before a stern Tribunal, and must reap
E'en as their days have sown! — (²) I could but
weep
O'er noble Minds which were perchance abused
By Spite or jealous Rancour, but there creep,
Like vipers i' the sun, a brood that used
Amiss the Mind's bright gift! — These, *these* have I
accused!

(¹) Dead.
(²) — "for whatsoever a man *soweth*, that shall he also *reap*."
[*Galatians : Chap. VI; v.* 7.

𝔅𝔶𝔯𝔬𝔫.

ONE will I single from the stern array
Of foes that throng around me — *one* whose hand
Stabb'd with a coward's skill!   Not through Life's
day,
But in his Mind's last midnight had she plann'd
This scheme of strange Ambition which hath
fann'd   [bear
The flames of fierce Contention! (¹) Though she
The sacred name of Woman I will brand
Base Shame upon her railings that the 'share (²)
Of Time shall *not* efface, nor canker'd Falsehood wear! (³)

(¹) " The best laid schemes o' mice an' men
Gang aft a-gley," etc.   [*Burns' " To a Mouse."*
Neither here, nor elsewhere, do I accuse this person of *malice aforethought.*
(²) Ploughshare.
(³) Regarding Byron's ability, *while living*, to cope with all adversaries, I append Shelley's powerful words : —
" The herded wolves, bold only to pursue ;

CANTO II.

𝕭𝖞𝖗𝖔𝖓.

THOU who art Crime's Avenger! (¹) it is thine
   To justify the Right! Ne'er yet, unheard,   [vine
With thee the guiltless plead! Here, where the
O'ermantles grim Decay, and the sage Bird
Of Night alone proclaims her plaintive word
O'er regal Desolation — where *he* stood,
The heavy-hearted " Pilgrim " long-deferr'd
From love that was his due — *here* shall the flood
Of Retribution rise, invoking blood for blood!

> The obscene ravens, clamorous o'er the dead;
> The vultures, to the conqueror's banner true,
> Who feed where Desolation first has fed,
> And whose wings rain contagion; how they fled,
> When like Apollo, from his golden bow,
> The Pythian of the age one arrow sped,
> And smiled! The spoilers tempt no second blow;
> They fawn on the proud feet that spurn them as they go."
> [*Shelley's "Adonais."*

(¹) Nemesis.

CANTO II.

Byron.

STERN Justice bared my blade! — Let me be just!
I would not swell, one *jot*, ([1]) her deed de-
plor'd! — ([2])
I will not swerve, one *tittle*, from my trust! [Sword,
Vengeance, which smiteth with Truth's two-edg'd
Shall scathe her as the Lightnings of the Lord! —
Have then the Dead no voice, and must they be
The spoil of each foul whisper — the abhorr'd
Defamers of our dust? Alas! that we [free! ([3])
Should have forsook our trust — first birthright of the

([1]) "For verily I say unto you, Till heaven and earth pass, one *jot* or one *tittle* shall in nowise pass from the law, till all be fulfilled."
         ,   [*St. Matthew: Chap. V; v. 18.*

([2]) "The accusing spirit, which flew up to heaven's chancery with the oath,

---

([3]) Men of England and America — ye who are my judges — answer! Shall the fame of our great Poet be transmitted to posterity sullied by this black re-proach? "No!" I hear your universal sentence, "let it perish in oblivion, for, surviving, it must ever cast a shade upon that Nation's honor it insulted, and whose sense of justice and propriety it so grossly violated."

CANTO II.

𝔅𝔶𝔯𝔬𝔫.

W HAT! was the Land of Washington he loved —
A Land he loved and honor'd as his own, — (¹)
(The foster-child of Freedom, who had proved
To her, as Greece, that love by deeds alone), —
Was *she* the first to cast the Pharisee's stone, (²)

---

blushed as he gave it in; and the recording angel, as he wrote it down, dropped a
tear upon the word and blotted it out forever." [*Sterne.*

(¹) "Can tyrants but by tyrants conquer'd be,
   And Freedom find no champion and no child
   Such as Columbia saw arise when she
   Sprung forth a Pallas, arm'd and undefiled?
   Or must such minds be nourish'd in the wild,
   Deep in the unpruned forest, 'midst the roar
   Of cataracts, where nursing Nature smiled
   On infant Washington? Has Earth no more
Such seeds within her breast, or Europe no such shore?"
   [*Byron's " Childe Harold:"   Canto IV; Stanza XCVI.*
      [*Continued on next page.*]

(²) "So, when they continued asking him, he lifted up himself, and said unto
them, He that is without sin among you, let him first *cast a stone* at her."
      [*St. John: Chap. VIII; v. 7.*

CANTO II.

And brand Dishonor on a deathless name?
Scorch'd be the scorpion tongue! — its harvest
sown (¹)
From winds reap Whirlwinds of eternal shame, (²)
And, o'er that damning page, Scorn breathe her wither-
ing flame! (³)

" And such they are — and such they will be found :
      Not so Leonidas and Washington,
      Whose every battle-field is holy ground,
      Which breathes of nations saved, not worlds undone.
      How sweetly on the ear such echoes sound !
      While the mere victor's may appal or stun
      The servile and the vain, such names will be
      A watchword till the future shall be free."
                    [*Byron's " Don Juan:" Canto VIII; Stanza V.*

(¹) [M.S. " Sear'd be the serpent tongue ! — its harvest sown," etc. — E.]

(²) "For they have sown the *wind,* and they shall reap the *whirlwind.*"
                                        [*Hosea : Chap. VIII; v.* 7.

(³) "Lord, who shall abide in thy tabernacle? who shall dwell in thy holy hill?
He that walketh uprightly, and worketh righteousness, and speaketh the truth
in his heart.
    He that backbiteth not with his tongue, nor doeth evil to his neighbour, nor
taketh up a reproach against his neighbour."   [*Psalms, XIV; v.* 1, 2, 3.
    "Thou shalt not go up and down as a tale-bearer among thy people; neither
shalt thou stand against the blood of thy neighbour : I am the Lord."
                                        [*Leviticus : Chap. XIX; v.* 16.

CANTO II.

𝕭𝖞𝖗𝖔𝖓.

"**M**ERCY is for the merciful!" (¹)　Ah, not in vain,
Great Nemesis! "The Pilgrim's" prayer arose
At thy sublimest shrine! — that cry of pain
Hath found a fitting echo — one that shows
Man may not all forsake what God hath chose
To sanctify as holy! — Hath Shame not
Reverted on *her* head? — those cruel blows,
Wherewith she sought to stain by one foul blot
A bleeding reputation, fallen to *her* lot? — (²)

(¹) " Lines on hearing that Lady Byron was ill."

(²) "Even in the afternoon of her best days;" etc.
　　　[*Shakespeare's* "*King Richard III:*" *Act III; Scene VII.*

" And thou, who never yet of human wrong
　Left the unbalanced scale, great Nemesis !
　Here, where the ancient paid thee homage long —
　Thou, who didst call the Furies from the abyss,
　And round Orestes bade them howl and hiss
　For that unnatural retribution — just,
　Had it but been from hands less near — in this
　Thy former realm, I call thee from the dust !
Dost thou not hear my heart? — Awake ! thou shalt, and must.

𝕭𝖞𝖗𝖔𝖓.

"ON her and hers," (¹) for lo! a Priest of Heaven,
    Wept by the World as Wolf of his own Fold,
Attests Time's awful vengeance! — (²)   Yea, the
    leaven

" It is not that I may not have incurr'd
For my ancestral faults or mine the wound
I bleed withal, and, had it been conferr'd
With a just weapon, it had flow'd unbound;
But now my blood shall not sink in the ground;
To thee I do devote it — *thou* shalt take
The vengeance, which shall yet be sought and found,
Which if *I* had not taken for the sake ——
But let that pass — I sleep, but thou shalt yet awake."
[*Byron's " Childe Harold :" Canto IV; Stanzas CXXXII, CXXXIII.*

(¹)   — " and I leave my curse
On her and hers forever! — "
                    [*Byron's " Marino Faliero :" Act V; Scene III.*

(²) " Unnatural deeds do breed unnatural troubles; infected minds to their
deaf pillows will discharge their secrets."
                    [*Shakespeare's " Macbeth :" Act V; Scene I.*

    I clip the following from the " Eastern Argus," published in Portland,
Maine, U. S. A. : —

CANTO II.

Of ruthless deeds will rise (^{1}) though Love seem
cold
And Justice' self insensate as the mould
That shrouds her voiceless victim; yet, at last,
Truth's trumpet-tone shall speak, and men behold
Each great Wrong righted — each Pretender cast,
Stripp'd of the Garb of Grace, (^{2}) all naked to the
blast! (^{3})

" —————.

The following by Whittier, quoted by ——— at the close of his argument,
says about all anybody will care to say of ——— : —

      " So fallen! so lost! the light withdrawn
      Which once he wore!
      The glory of his gray hairs gone
      Forevermore!

      " Revile him not! the Tempter hath
      A snare for all,
      And pitying tears, not Scorn and Wrath
      Befit his fall.   *[Next page.]*

(^{1})   "Foul deeds will rise,
      Though all the Earth o'erwhelm them, to men's eyes."
             [Shakespeare's " *Hamlet :* " *Act I; Scene II.*

(^{2}) "Robes, and furr'd gowns, hide all. Plate sin with gold,

---

(^{3}) " What a fool is he who locks his door to keep out spirits, who has in his

𝕭𝖞𝖗𝖔𝖓.

FAREWELL! ye harpy horde! I could forgive,
But some are past Forgiveness! This, my verse,
Shall sink into men's hearts, and years but give
My page a deeper meaning to rehearse
This Drama of the Past! There sleeps no curse

" O, dumb be Passion's stormy rage,
   When he who might
Have lighted up and led his Age,
   Falls back in Night.

" Scorn! would the Angels laugh, to mark
   A bright Soul driven,
Fiend-goaded, down the endless dark,
   From Hope and Heaven?

" Let not the Land once proud of him
   Insult him now,
Nor brand, with deeper shame, his dim,
   Dishonored brow!   [*Next page.*]

And the strong lance of justice hurtless breaks;
Arm it in rags, a pygmy's straw doth pierce it."
   [*Shakespeare's " King Lear :" Act IV ; Scene VI.*

---

own bosom a spirit he dares not meet alone; whose voice, smothered far down, and

CANTO II.

More awful than the Voice of Conscience! — this,
This shall my line awake! — thou dusky nurse
That brood'st o'er guilty bosoms,(¹) I dismiss
To thee such faithless Souls unfit to share Love's bliss!

" But let its humbled sons, instead,
　From sea to lake,
' 　A long lament, as for the dead,
　In sadness make.

" Of all we loved and honored, naught
　Save Power remains,
　A fallen Angel's pride of thought,
　Still strong in chains.

" All else is gone : from those great eyes
　The Soul has fled :
When Faith is lost, when Honor dies,
　The man is dead ! "

　　　　[*John G. Whittier.* (¹)

(¹) Although these lines were originally written upon another, justice demands that we should " Render unto Cæsar the things which are Cæsar's."

piled over with mountains of earthliness, is yet like the forewarning trumpet of doom !"　　　　[*Harriet Beecher Stowe.*

— " there is no future pang
Can deal that justice on the self-condemn'd
He deals on his own soul."

　　　　[*Byron's* " *Manfred :* " *Act III; Scene I.*

(¹) " Every man's *conscience* is a thousand swords," etc.

　　[*Shakespeare's* " *King Richard III :* " *Act V; Scene III.*

𝕮𝖎𝖗𝖈𝖚𝖘 𝕸𝖆𝖝𝖎𝖒𝖚𝖘.

WHILOM the mighty Circus curv'd afar
  Its massy wall, now levell'd with the dust! —
Flew the fleet courser! — glanc'd the glittering
  car! —
Swell'd the deep shout of Triumph or Disgust! —
While half a million graced the glorious just, (¹)
And all apace the mad excitement grew! —
Tyrants applauded with a thirsty lust,
Seeking the semblance of a pleasaunce (²) new!
Such shone the splendrous scene with many a shifting
  hue! (³)

(¹) Also written *joust.*

(²) Pleasaunce — pleasure. — " Faire-seemely *pleasaunce* each to other makes,"
etc.   [*Spenser's " Faerie Queene:*" Book I; Canto II.

(³) [M. S. "Such shone the splendrous scene, charg'd with chameleon
hue!" — E.]

CANTO II.

Circus Maximus.

L OW lie thy Towers of Strength! — Thy Walls of
Pride! —
Throned Palaces that lined thy long expanse
Where swell'd the living surge, till the loud tide
Of clamorous acclaim rous'd from his trance —
The Banquet and the Bowl — he whose haught
glance
Bade the bold sports begin! — his kerchief
waves! — (¹)
At which sweet sight proud-snorting steeds advance,
While with the word — the sign each stallion
craves —   [slaves!
The thrilling start is made! — Rejoice! Lust's loving

(¹) When the clamors of the people had reached a great height, it was the custom
of Nero to cast his handkerchief from the window of the adjoining Palace where
he sate at banquet; by which signal, permission was granted for the sports of the
Circus to begin.

𝕮ircus 𝕸aximus. [1]

HERE urg'd his steeds the flying Charioteer! —
He nears the goal, and thrice ten thousand throats
Salute the Victor, as in mad career
The gallant brutes strain every nerve, and floats
Each free mane on the wind! — the Conqueror gloats
O'er the rich prize he may, in fancy, clasp! —
'Tis won! 'Tis won! — the gain on which he doats
Shall soon be his! — how the wild coursers gasp —
Aha! it matters not, — *the palm is in his grasp!*

---

[1] "Le grande cirque occupait entre les monts Aventin et Palatin un espace allongé de 2400 pieds de longueur sur 450 de large, commençant à quelque distance du Tibre, près la place Bocca della Verità. Il pouvait, au temps de Vespasien, qui l'agrandit, contenir 250,000 spectateurs, et, sous Constantin, près de 400,000. On y donnait des jeux dits circenses, consistant en luttes d'athlètes, en courses à pied, à cheval, en chars, etc."

[*Du Pays.*

CANTO II.

𝔖𝔱. 𝔓𝔢𝔱𝔢𝔯'𝔰.

A ND thou — cloud-cleaving and resplendent dome! —
  High shrine of the Almighty! (') I behold
Again thy mimic Heaven! — once more may roam
'Neath its colossal span — the mightiest mould
Of Man's inspir'd creation — where, unroll'd,
Thy matchless magnitude beyond me soars,
Piercing the sapphire vault as if to hold
Converse with the Eternal! Let us pause,
St. Peter's! at thy plinth, before the mystic Cause,

(') " The hand that rounded Peter's dome,
  And groined the aisles of Christian Rome,
  Wrought in a sad sincerity;
  Himself from God he could not free;
  He builded better than he knew; —
  The conscious stone to beauty grew."
                    [*Emerson's " Problem.*"

St. Peter's.[1]

TO ask why thou wert rear'd — why men have made
A God unto themselves, crowning their days
With sweet heart-offerings? Not till thou shalt
    fade,
O, Sun of papal Splendour! and thy rays
Pale as the dim forgotten, mock the blaze
Of that which now thou art — nay! till thy site
Be of great things unknown — until decays
Each instinct of the Mind, and utter Night
Brood o'er the blighted Earth, may aught oppugn His
    might!

---

[1] "La longueur du temple est de 575 pieds; celle de la nef transversale, de 417; la largeur de la grande nef du milieu est de 87 pieds, et on compte 142 pieds du pavé jusqu'à la voûte. Les deux anges enfantins qui soutiennent les béniticrs en marbe n'ont pas moins de 6 pieds. — Cette basilique est à croix latine et à trois nefs; celle du milieu est divisée par huit gros piliers qui soutiennent quatre grands arcs de chaque côté: ceux-ci répondent à autant de chapelles. A chacun des piliers sont adossés deux pilastres cannelés d'ordre corinthien, qui

CANTO II.

$t. $eter's.

W HO shall unfold the Future? Centuries
Have run their varying round since He arose,
The lowly Nazarene, who framed decrees
For princely Potentates, and o'er the woes
Of flesh spake still triumphant in the close
Of His immortal mission, with a glance
Of that exalted Prophecy which throws
Its gleam o'er generations whose expanse,
To Inspiration's eye, teems with significance.

---

ont 8 pieds de largeur et 77 de hauteur, y compris la base et le chapiteau; ils
soutiennent un entablement de 18 pieds de hauteur, qui règne tout autour de
l'église. Entre les pilastres sont deux rangs de niches; celles du bas renferment
des statues de marbre, de 15 pieds. Sur chacun des grands arcs sont deux figures
en stuc, de 15 pieds de haut, représentant des Vertus. Les contre-pilastres qui
correspondent sous les arcs sont ornés de deux médaillons, soutenus séparément
par deux enfants de marbre blanc aux formes molles et rebondies; ces médaillons
renferment les portraits de différents papes. Entre ces médaillons on voit deux
autre enfants portant les attributs pontificaux; le tout a été sculpté en bas-reliefs
sous la direction du Bernin. La grande voûte de l'eglise est décorée de caissons
á rosaces en stuc doré. Le pavé fut formé de beaux marbres, sous la direction de
Jacques de la Porte et du *Bernin.* 	*	*	*	*	*	*	*	*

St. Peter's.

UNTO this man, or God — albeit which
    The world holds hot dispute — hast thou been
    rais'd,
  O, Christ's enthron'd Cathedral! to enrich,
  As a Queen Jewel, the starr'd crown that blaz'd
  O'er Popish Majesty! — Indeed amaz'd
  Had been the humble fisherman whose name
  Thou bear'st, stupendous Pile — could he have
    gazed
  On those transcendent glories that became
The Synonym of Power — the Harbinger of Fame!

Cette immense façade en travertin n'a pas moins de 370 pieds de largeur et 149 de hauteur. Les huit colonnes corinthiennes, qui, vues de l'obélisque, paraissent si petites, ont 88 pieds d'élévation et 8 pieds 5 pouces de diamètre. L'attique est couronnée de 18 statues colossales (Jésus-Christ et les Apôtres), de 17 pieds de haut. Aux extrémités sont *deux horloges*, dessinées par l'architecte Valadier et placées sous Pie VI (l'une marque les heures à l'italienne). On entre

𝕻𝖆𝖙𝖎𝖈𝖆𝖓. (¹)

THE Prince of Palaces beams on our sight! —
The treasure-house of Learning and of Art! —
The Vatican, where rescued from the Night
Of perish'd Ages pines a beauteous part
Of the too-beauteous Past! — spread, like a chart,
Before the dazzl'd vision we essay
To trace to its far fount " The mighty Heart," (²)
Whose fluttering pulse-beats, quickening to Decay,
Enchain, but cheat the sense, by Beauty's blinding ray! —

par cinq portes dans un magnifique portique de 47 pieds de largeur et de 439 pieds
de longueur, y compris les vestibules des extrémités, et l'on voit les statues éques-
tres de Constantin le Grand, par le *Bernin* et de Charlemagne, par *Cornacchini.*"
                                                                          [*Du Pays.*

(¹) "Le Vatican, — capitole de la Rome moderne, est moins un palais qu'une
réunion de palais, d'édifices irréguliers auxquels travaillèrent les plus célèbres
architectes, *Bramante (Raphaël), Pirro Ligorio, Dominique Fontana, Charles
Maderne, Bernin.* — Il est à trois étages, renferme une infinité de salles, de gal-

(²) *Byron's " Childe Harold:" Canto IV; Stanza LXXXVIII.*

𝕍𝖆𝖙𝖎𝖈𝖆𝖓.

A BEAUTY now no more, save through this gleam
   That permeates the Present in such shapes —
Fair Children of the Chisel — the fond dream
Of each God-gifted Genius who escapes,
Perchance, Time's transient tablet which but
   drapes,
With Memory's green garland, the bright name
His bays bequeath'd high Art; but, from the apes
Of stern Sublimity, her face, for shame,
Rome's grief-worn Goddess veils! — quench'd is her
   ancient flame!

---

cries, de chapelles, de corridors, une bibliothèque, un musée immense, un jardin;
on y compte 20 cours, 8 grands escaliers et 200 escaliers de service. Bonanni
(Templi vaticani historia) prétend que le Vatican contient 13,000 chambres, en y
comprenant les souterrains. Ce qui manque à ce vaste ensemble de bâtiments,
c'est une façade extérieure. Du côté par où on l'aborde, il est masqué par la
colonnade de la place de Saint Pierre."   [*Du Pays.*

CANTO II.

𝕮atacombs. (¹)

THOU City of the Dead! — the dreary seat
Of Death and Desolation! May these be
The men that tamed the Proud, and thrall'd the
  Great? —
Why! *Time* out-cæsars Cæsar! — (²) his decree
Hath levell'd Prince with Peasant! — lo! we see
All one! — perchance the Conqueror's crumbling
  mound
May crown some statelier cell, but now no knee
Bends in forc'd adulation, nor is found,
On Earth, one far-fled shadow of their vantage-ground!

(¹) "Les Catacombes de Rome s'étendent dans diverses directions autour des remparts de la ville et dans la campagne. On en connaît une soixantaine, et on estime qu'il en existe trois fois plus à découvrir. Elles forment un dédale de chemins souterrains, de corridors étroits et bas, présentant de distance en distance les espèces de chambres carrées qui servaient d'oratoires aux chrétiens."

[*Du Pays.*

(²) — " it *out-herods* Herod."

[*Shakespeare's* " *Hamlet* : " *Act III; Scene II.*

Words of Parting.

MY strain draws nigh its close, but it hath been
 A not unwelcome task: what though its stream
 Be swoln by burning tears? — if Genius glean
 Aught from bow'd Torture's teachings — blend one
  beam
 With her Cæsarean crown — in sooth Hope's dream
 Of high Ambition hath not vied in vain! (¹)
 I may not live to mark men laud my theme,
 Nor cozening critics question, nor remain
The sick spectator of a wanton World's disdain

(¹) " All this hath somewhat worn me, and may wear,
 But must be borne. I stoop not to despair ;
 For I have battled with mine agony,
 And made me wings wherewith to overfly
 The narrow circus of my dungeon wall," etc.
    [*Byron's " Lament of Tasso."*

CANTO II.

Words of Parting.

THOUGH such should be accorded as my meed! —
I' faith I care not! for Fame hath become,
To these young eyes, a harvest sown of seed
Whose bloom is Barrenness: not for full sum
Of hollow Approbation, nor hot hum
Of Mammon's myriads in blood-bought applause,
Would I unbend my Being, but were dumb. —
I clasp'd Fray's falchion in *another's* cause —
That blade, though bathed with blood, was bared by
Love's bright laws! (¹)

(¹) "Love took up the harp of Life, and smote on all the chords
　　　with might;
　　Smote the chord of Self, that, trembling, passed in music
　　　out of sight."

[*Tennyson's " Locksley Hall."*
"Let fame go —

𝔚𝔬𝔯𝔡𝔰 𝔬𝔣 𝔓𝔞𝔯𝔱𝔦𝔫𝔤.

S TILL it may be I have not sung in vain,
 Nor sown Hope's seed to ashes: hence shall
  flood,
 Perchance, a band of warriors, but refrain
 From dark self-slaughter of the Dragon's brood, ([1])

I care not much what shall become of fame,
So I save love and do mine own soul right;" etc.
    [*Swinburne's "Chastelard:" Act IV; Scene I.*

([1]) " While Cadmus stood over his conquered foe, contemplating its vast size,
a voice was heard (from whence he knew not, but he heard it distinctly) com-
manding him to take the dragon's teeth and sow them in the earth. He obeyed.
He made a furrow in the ground, and planted the teeth, destined to produce a
crop of men. Scarce had he done so when the clods began to move, and the
points of spears appear above the surface. Next helmets with their nodding
plumes came up, and next the shoulders and breasts and limbs of men with
weapons, and in time a harvest of armed warriors. Cadmus alarmed prepared
to encounter a new enemy, but one of them said to him, ' Meddle not with our
civil war.' With that he who had spoken smote one of his earth-born brothers
with a sword, and he himself fell pierced with an arrow from another. The latter
fell a victim to a fourth, and in like manner the whole crowd dealt with each

CANTO II.

Turning their arms, unstain'd with brothers' blood,
'Gainst the pale Vampires of the peaceful Grave!(¹)
The issue bides with Heaven! If, from this bud,
A Flower of Beauty spring, (²) fair shall it wave
Though he that loved it lie, calm, in his clay-cold cave!(³)

---

other till all fell slain with mutual wounds, except five survivors. One of these
cast away his weapons and said, 'Brothers, let us live in peace!' These five
joined with Cadmus in building his city, to which he gave the name of Thebes."
                                   [" *The Age of Fable ;* " *Bulfinch.*

(¹) [M.S. " 'Gainst the gaunt Prowlers of th' unguarded Grave ! " — E.]

(²) " This bud of love, by Summer's ripening breath,
      May prove a beauteous flower when next we meet."
                 [*Shakespeare's* " *Romeo and Juliet :* " *Act II; Scene II.*

(³)   " — and what if thou withdraw
      In silence from the living, and no friend
      Take note of thy departure? All that breathe
      Will share thy destiny. The gay will laugh
      When thou art gone, the solemn brood of care
      Plod on, and each one, as before, will chase
      His favorite phantom ; yet all these shall leave
      Their mirth and their employments, and shall come
      And make their bed with thee."
                               [*Bryant's* " *Thanatopsis.*"

𝔚𝔬𝔯𝔡𝔰 𝔬𝔣 𝔓𝔞𝔯𝔱𝔦𝔫𝔤.

FAREWELL! — Fierce floods, that bore 'pon their
broad breast
Me and my bark as bubbles, ebb away!
Now fleet-wing'd Fancy flies her humble nest,
Leaving me, lonely, 'mid this Curse of Clay; (¹)
Feeling all past Peace wreck'd, the Future's ray
Bound by black thralls that threat pale Peril's
path —
Weird-beck'ning Aspects which would blast my
way —
Semblance of shapes that were: Ambition's
wraith, [faith!
And the sweet shade of Love, scoff at mine ancient

(¹) " ' For here, forlorn and lost, I tread
With fainting steps and slow —

CANTO II.

Words of Parting.

SO be it! If Earth bear no further fruit,
I rank Remembrance, bitter though it be,
Hope's holiest heritage, like some sweet lute
Breathing long-buried sorrows o'er Life's sea
From the lull'd Past, until, 'yond (¹) that far lee,
Swelling against those winds wherewith I strive,
Comes, calm and clear, an echo full and free —
Light siren-songs which woo'd, with Love's gay
  gyve,
My fond, o'er-ardent Youth! — feelings years may not
  rive! (²)

Where wilds, immeasurably spread,
Seem lengthening as I go.' "
    [*Goldsmith's "Hermit."*

(¹) Beyond.
(²) " When to the sessions of sweet silent thought
  I summon up remembrance of things past," etc.
    [*Shakespeare's " Sonnet XXX."*

𝔚𝔬𝔯𝔡𝔰 𝔬𝔣 𝔓𝔞𝔯𝔱𝔦𝔫𝔤.

A FOND Farewell!—Aye! thou dear theme, Adieu!
Meeting mere strangers, as sad playmates press
The hallow'd hand at parting, to renew
Their wide-dividing ways through Wilderness,
Sun, Storm, or Shadow — wilds which blast or
    bless —
Press we the Palm of Friendship!([1]) Thoughts
    wax things
Of individual Essence, nor live less
Than those bright Beings that inspire the springs
Of Poesy's sweet strain with Pegasean wings!

([1]) —— "while o'er the brim of life's beaker I dip,
    Though the cup may next moment be shatter'd, the
      wine
    Spilt, one deep health I'll pledge, and that health
      shall be thine," etc.
               [*Owen Meredith's* "*Lucile:*" *Part I; Canto V.*

𝔉𝔞𝔯𝔢𝔴𝔢𝔩𝔩.

MY forge-lights flicker 'bove a fading brand —
Hoar, stark and soulless, for all flame hath fled! —
Its last spark is extinguish'd! — lo! the hand
That fashion'd it, now nerveless as the dead,
Drops its weak grasp! — with a dull load, like
   lead,
Existence *aches* upon me! — I awake,
The old, unalter'd Being, that for bread
Receiv'd from men a stone — for fish a snake! (¹)
Truth's deathless triumph dawns! — Time shall stern
   vengeance take! (²)

(¹) " Or what man is there of you, whom if his son ask bread, will he give him
a *stone!* Or if he ask a fish, will he give him a *serpent!* "
                              [*St. Matthew : Chap. VII; v. 9, 10.*
(²) The concluding line refers not to myself, but to him I defend.

Hymn to Mt. Blanc.

Hymn to the Ocean.

Hymn to Mt. Blanc.

MAJESTIC Monarch of the mountain-cloud!
Proud Prophet! Ye whose scarr'd, sky-towering
   top
Is lifted 'bove thy kindred — lost in air!
From whose veil'd bosom to the void below,
Deaf'ning descendeth, ever and anon,
The frozen Torrent of the Avalanche
With torn and thund'rous echoes from afar!
Along whose haught and bleak, bolt-riven brow
The awful Hand of Time hath Ages lain!
Scath'd Prince of Pride! brave-scarr'd and beaten
By the Tempest's wrath!
                                    From whose icy heart

The mountain brooklet leaps with wild, mad joy,
From crag to crag, into the gulf beneath!
Lo, do I love Ye!   On my knees I bow,
And lift my Soul, in ecstasy, to Thee,
Lone Hierarch!

List! from the peaceful plain
Soft-tinkling herd-bells of the shepherd's fold
Rise on the gentle wind in fairy chime,
Whilst mournful mem'ries of departed days
Drift, dreamlike, 'pon the placid ev'ning air.
Far, far aloft, along Thy fields of snow,
The full-orb'd Moon hath pour'd her pallid flood;
There, soaring silent through Thy silv'ry shroud,
Thou seek'st communion with the starry Night!
Yea! do I love Ye 'neath blest Dian's beam —

When warm Aurora, budding o'er Thy brow,
Doth dye with purple kisses Thy pale front! —
Then art Thou fair as on that first, far day
When Thou wert moulded by the Master's hand!

O, Answer! what is Man?
                                     Stupendous Pile!
If I, as Thee, might wanton with the Clouds,
Or garb me in the Glories of the Night,
Or bind the Rainbow's Chaplet round my brow,
Methinks I still were happy, since with me
Mere love or hate of *Man* must link with naught! —
Then were my mates the Lightning and the Storm —
My wrath, rous'd Jove's red-wing'd Artillery —
E'en at my feet each star-crown'd crag should fall,
Shaking the firm-set Earth to her fix'd base! —

I'd crave compactures with the wandering Winds,
Or force from them their tale of bastard birth —
Their errand — whence they came — e'en WHO
commands!

O, Christ! lone Crags, I love Ye! — Yea! my Soul,
Cleft, wrung, rebellious, doth defy control —
Sets her haught heel upon the writhing worm
That cribs her in this Charnel-house of Clay! —
Avaunt! the thought is Madness! — *I* AM *THINE!*

Hymn to the Ocean.

GRAND Anthem of Jehovah! Give Thee Hail!
O, Mighty One! Give Answer! On Thy wail,
That sounds forever from Thy farthest shore,
The deep Te Deum of ten thousand Psalms!
O, moanful music of the Lurley's lay,
The soft complainings of the Summer breeze
That sweetly slumbers 'pon Thy heaving breast,
Which, like a mother's, trembling at its touch,
Doth make Thy very fondness kin to pain!

Anon! behold! Thy peaceful sleep is broke,
And, like a chieftain on the battle-morn,
Thou risest, naked, to confront the Storm,

Or mov'st, majestic, 'neath His tyrant touch!
Then art Thou mighty!   Then are we that gaze
Upon Thee thrill'd — stirr'd to the Soul's deep spring
With awful whispers of that viewless God
Whose voice Thou and the lawless Winds obey!

O, boundless Waste of Waters! Soulless Solitude!
Wild waves eternal-rising crest on crest —
Forever-dying born to Life anew!

O, Mighty One!   Give Answer!   I would search
The secret shadow of Thy haunting pain!
Tell Thou of them deep-hid, forevermore,
Within Thy hollow heart's sarcophagi!
Tell to the loving wife, the tender maid,
Of him whose bones lie bleaching on Thy sands,

Unmeasur'd fathoms 'neath Thy breakers' din!
Poor wretch! devoted to Heaven's warring Gods!—
O'ertaken by the giant Whirlwind's wrath!
Tell of that rosy morn his sheeny sail
Bore yon lone wand'rer from the smiling shore,
When Thou did'st hearken to a fond wife's prayer
For prosp'rous voyage sped by gentle Winds!
Tell of the murk, black Night! The howling Storm!
Thine angry billows capt with yeasty foam!
The Lightning's glare! The Gale's wild lullaby!
The Heart's despair! The fierce, brief struggle!
And the freed Soul's flight to realms afar!
Ah! long, long ere those aching eyes shall greet
The husband, or the lover, far away;
For Thou, Most Mighty! mark'd him for Thine own,
Ere yet his boyhood 'gan Thy dread career!

O, Mighty One! Give Answer! I would search
The secret shadow of Thy haunting pain!
Why dost Thou raise, eternally, to God
Thy weary voice in hoarse lament that Thou wert
    made?
Alas! I know not — yet I know *my heart*
Doth yearn toward Thee, in Thy great agony;
For through its core the same strong pulse doth
    beat,
With an'all-ebbless tide, like unto Thine!
And I have sought Thee in Thy tender moods,
But Thou vouchsaf'd no answer! Worshipping,
Along Thy pebbl'd shore I've paced the Night,
Communing with Thy Spirit till the Dawn,
Then, weary, sought my couch to dream of Thee,
And come again to question and adore!

Oft, gazing on Thee 'neath the Crescent beam
Whose golden splendour kiss'd the silver sands
Beneath my feet, my Soul hath risen
From her Mask of Clay, and up the broad'ning vista
Ta'en her flight, and there hath seen and question'd
That which *other* men perchance may *dream*,
But none may *know!* Then, to my list'ning Soul,
Thy moan seem'd sweetest music, and the melody
Of Thy deep monotone — an awful requiem, —
Swell'd solemnly 'bove Thy still-sleeping host!

O, Mighty One! Give Answer! I would search
The secret shadow of Thy haunting pain!
Upon Thy shore I've mark'd Thee cast, contempt-
uously,
Thy warlike spoils, like as a wayward child

That wearied of its romp and boist'rous play,
Doth, sated, quit its toys to sigh for new!
Weird toys are Thine, that freeze, at its warm spring,
The genial flow in hearts of them that gaze! —
Old, riven planks, pierc'd by the sleepless worm —
Truss'd through by rusted spike, or grim, red bolt,
And garnish'd deep with fringe of waving moss
To which cling living shells that feast on Death! —
A half-effac'd inscription like a name —
The sole survivor of some stately ship
Whose sunken prow sleeps in Thy crystal tomb!
O, silent Tragedy! O, Actors hush'd in Death!
This, thy lone witness, comes from thee afar,
An hundred leagues, to tell thou art no more!

Ah! who shall pierce Thy sunless vault below? —

Who gaze upon that phantom barque which lies,
Slow-rotting, 'neath Thy dead and pulseless tide? —
The bony Steersman — spitted on his wheel —
A ghastly spectre, peering through the gloom
With hollow orbs, as if *it* would divine
The dreadful Aspect of Eternity?

Upon Thy boundless plain of shining sands
Bloom rare sea-plants, and Children of the Deep —
The crimson coral, which, with graceful spray,
Doth mock her frailer sisters born of Earth!
But, fairer far, those sweet and gentle flowers
That in Thy hauntless wilds unheeded blow
With wanton fragrance, save the Merman King
Doth seek, with them, his true-love's troth to plight!

Heap'd in Thy caves lies hid the glittering store
Bold men have wrested from the Womb of Earth;
But Thou did'st gripe it in Thine amorous clutch'
Who shall disputeless hoard, forevermore!

Thou art eternal, and shalt proudly roll
When millions be departed, yet unborn;—
Man's day a flower that at Life's Ev'ning fades,
To moulder 'neath the mute and senseless stone!
But, ah! the *Spirit*, striving in my breast,
Doth *there* Thy vaunted sov'reignty deny—
My Soul shall seek afar her " captain, Christ," (¹)
When Thou reced'st to Thy remotest shore!

Yet do I love Thee, and my deep delight

(¹) *Shakespeare's "King Richard II:" Act IV; Scene I.*

Is heark'ning to Thine angry surges' call, —
Thy rush of fury 'gainst the jagg'd, black rocks,—
The mutter'd thunder of Thy baffl'd roar!

Farewell! thou Marvel of an unseen God!
Farewell! O, Herald of perpetual Song!
Farewell! thou Burthen of ten thousand Psalms!
Grand Anthem of Jehovah! Give Farewell!